"You could come in for a coffee, if you like," she said.

It was tempting. So very tempting.

But it wouldn't be fair to her to start something that he knew he couldn't finish.

"Thanks, but…"

"But no thanks," she finished. "I understand."

But there had been a flash of hurt in her eyes. It made him want to make her feel better. And all his common sense went out of the window, because he wrapped his arms around her. Lowered his mouth to hers. Brushed his lips against hers once, twice…

Her hands were in his hair and she was kissing him back when he came to his senses again and broke the kiss.

"I'm sorry. That wasn't fair of me," he said. "I'm not in a position to date anyone. I have Iain to think of. If my situation was different, I'd ask you out properly."

"And I'd turn you down, because I'd still be concentrating on my career."

Whoever had hurt her had *really* hurt her, he thought.

"Message understood," he said. "Good night, Beatrice."

"Good night, Daniel."

And he turned away before he did something stupid. Like ask her to change both their minds.

Dear Reader,

What happens when you meet someone you really click with—but you've both been on opposite sides of the same difficult issue, so being together means you'll have to come to terms with the tragedy of your past?

Beatrice meets Daniel, a single dad whose child is the same age her daughter would've been had the car crash not happened. Daniel has sworn off relationships, wanting to protect his son and guard his own heart, but how can he resist someone as warm and kind and sweet as Beatrice? Beatrice has also sworn off relationships, not wanting to risk a repeat of her past. But as they get to know each other at work and find their mutual attraction too much to resist, they think they can move forward. Until their joint worst nightmare rears its head…

I hope you enjoy Beatrice and Daniel's story.

With love,

Kate Hardy

CARRYING THE SINGLE DAD'S BABY

KATE HARDY

HARLEQUIN® MEDICAL ROMANCE™

Recycling programs
for this product may
not exist in your area.

ISBN-13: 978-1-335-66372-6

Carrying the Single Dad's Baby

First North American Publication 2018

Copyright © 2018 by Pamela Brooks

Printed in U.S.A.

To my editors, Sheila and Megan, with love and
thanks for being so patient with me!

CHAPTER ONE

EMERGENCY DEPARTMENT.

The letters stood out, white on a blue background. Just the same as they had in the last hospital where Beatrice had worked.

Except at Muswell Hill Memorial Hospital she would be getting a fresh start. This was a new place, where nobody knew about her past, so nobody could pity her. Not for her divorce, not for the baby, not for the way her life had totally imploded four years ago.

They'd all see her for who she was now. Beatrice Lindford, the new emergency consultant. Beatrice who was cool, calm and perfectly controlled. Who led her team from the front. And who'd baked brownies the night before to say hello to her new department.

She took a deep breath, pushed open the

swing doors with her free hand, and walked into the reception area.

Michael Harcourt, the head of the department, was waiting for her.

'Beatrice, lovely that you made it. Come and meet the team.' He looked quizzically at her. 'What's in the boxes?'

'Home-made brownies. Just my way of saying hello to everyone.'

'You didn't have to bring anything,' he said with a smile, 'but they'll go down very well in the staff kitchen. Now, let me find someone to show you round… Ah, Josh.' He called over one of the younger doctors. 'Josh, I think you're rostered in Resus with Beatrice, our new consultant, this morning. I'd like you to show her round before it all gets hectic.'

Was it her imagination, or was Josh looking at her slightly oddly?

'Beatrice, this is Josh, one of our juniors. He's a good lad, but don't ever let him drive you anywhere—unless you don't mind risking ending up with a tension pneumothorax, eh, Josh?' Chuckling, Michael walked away.

Josh groaned. 'Please don't take too much notice of what the boss just said. My pneumothorax was months ago, and it was only because I wasn't used to go-karting on ice and I took the corner too fast.'

'Go-karting on *ice*?' Beatrice raised an eyebrow. That sounded like the definition of insanity, to her.

'Sam—he's one of the registrars and you'll meet him shortly—thought it would be a good team-building exercise,' Josh explained. 'And it was. It was great fun. Except I, um, crashed. And nobody's ever going to let me forget it. Ever.' He groaned again. 'Even in the Christmas secret Santa last year, I got a modified model motorcycle.'

She smiled. 'Oh, dear. So Sam's a bit of a daredevil?'

Josh smiled back. 'He used to be. He's changed a bit, now he's a dad.'

Babies.

Of course people in the department would have babies and small children. The same as they would anywhere she worked.

She wasn't going to let it throw her. This was about her job, not her personal life.

'Can we start with the staff kitchen so I can drop these off?' She indicated the plastic boxes she was carrying.

'Sure.' He looked interested. 'What's in them?'

'Brownies.' The recipe they used at Beresford Castle that had actually got a write-up in one of the Sunday supplements, and made all the tourists come back for more. 'I hope I made enough for everyone working in the department today.'

'You made them yourself?'

'Last night.' With a bit of help from her niece and nephews.

'That's a lot of work. And it's really nice of you.'

'Just my way of saying hello to my new team,' she said with a smile. 'And I was planning on buying everyone a drink tonight after my shift, if you can maybe recommend somewhere. I've only just moved here, so I don't really know the area yet.'

'The Red Lion, just round the corner, is fairly popular,' he said.

'The Red Lion it is, then,' she said.

Once they'd dropped the boxes of brownies in the staff kitchen, with a note she'd written earlier propped against them inviting the team to help themselves, Josh showed her round the department and introduced her to the team.

Everyone seemed friendly enough, but when a doctor strode out of cubicles, clearly ready to see his next patient, Josh suddenly looked awkward. 'Um, and this is Daniel Capaldi, one of the registrars. Daniel, this is Beatrice Lindford, our new...' His voice trailed off.

Why was Josh suddenly acting like a cat on a hot tin roof? Beatrice wondered. What was it about Daniel Capaldi that had made the junior doctor so nervous?

Quite apart from the fact that Daniel looked as if he could've graced the pages of a high-end glossy fashion magazine; she didn't think she'd ever met anyone so good-looking in her entire life. He was tall enough for her to have to look up to him, with dark hair brushed back from his forehead—the type of hair that would curl when it was wet—dark eyes, the longest eyelashes she'd ever seen on a man, and a mouth with an incredibly sensual curve.

He was breathtakingly beautiful.

Maybe he was the type who knew just how good-looking he was, and was used to women falling at his feet. Well, she didn't care what her colleagues looked like. She just wanted them to be good at their jobs, communicate properly and work with her as a team to give their patients the best care possible. She wasn't interested in anything else. Not any more.

'Beatrice Lindford, the newest member of the team,' she said coolly, and held out her hand to shake his.

What she hadn't expected was the tingle all the way down her spine when Daniel took her hand and shook it firmly. She couldn't even remember the last time she'd reacted so strongly to anyone.

Not good.

Really not good.

Because she didn't want to get involved with anyone. Ever again.

Beatrice Lindford. The new consultant. The one who'd just been appointed to the job everyone had thought had Daniel's name on it. A job that part of Daniel had wanted; but part of him hadn't, because he knew he couldn't give the department what it needed from him in that role at the same time as being a good single parent to Iain.

If things had been different with Jenny, he wouldn't have hesitated to apply for the job.

But it was pointless dwelling on might-have-beens. The situation was as it was. Jenny was remarried now—to someone else.

He had custody of Iain. And his son would always, always come first.

Beatrice wasn't what Daniel had expected. She was tall, maybe four inches shorter than his own six foot two. Almost white-blonde hair that she wore tied back with a scarf at the nape of her neck. The bluest eyes he'd ever seen—the colour of the sky on a late summer evening. And an incredibly posh accent, which made her his polar opposite: clearly she came from a privileged background, whereas Daniel was the son of a teenage mum who'd been brought up mainly by his grandparents until his mother was able to cope with being a parent. They were worlds apart.

But the bit that really threw him was when he shook her hand. That handshake was meant to be businesslike, maybe even slightly on the cool side. Instead, it felt as if every single nerve ending in his body had just woken up. He'd never been so physically aware of anyone before.

Absolutely not.

Even if Beatrice Lindford was single, and even if she was interested in him, he wasn't in the market for a relationship. Iain was his world, and that was the way it was going to stay.

And he wanted a bit of distance between himself and Beatrice until he could get himself perfectly back under control and treat her just like any other member of the department, instead of behaving like a teenager who'd just felt the heady pull of sexual attraction for the first time in his life.

'Welcome to the department, Ms Lindford,' he said, giving her a cool nod. 'Josh, shouldn't you be in Resus?'

'As should I,' Beatrice said, narrowing her eyes slightly at him. 'Michael Harcourt asked Josh to show me round and introduce me to everyone, and he's been kind enough to do just that.'

He liked the fact that she'd stood up for the junior doctor. But he didn't want to like Beatrice Lindford. He wanted to keep his distance from her, at least until he could get this unwanted attraction under control. 'Indeed,' he said.

'There are brownies in the staff kitchen,' she said. 'Do help yourself.'

There was a touch of haughtiness to her voice. She sounded for all the world as if she'd just taken over their department.

Which, he supposed, she sort of had, being their new consultant. 'Thank you,' he said.

'And I'm buying drinks at the Red Lion after my shift,' she said.

Drinks he definitely wouldn't be going to. 'Noted.'

'I guess Josh and I had better get back to Resus.'

Daniel knew he hadn't been particularly friendly to his new colleague, and he felt slightly guilty about that. But his response to her had flustered him, and right now there was no room in his life for anything other than his son. 'Uh-huh,' he said, and turned away.

Daniel hadn't been openly hostile, but there had definitely been something there. Beatrice couldn't understand what the problem was. They'd never met each other before or even knew of each other by reputation. Or was Daniel just offhand like that with everyone, and that was why Josh had looked so awkward before he'd introduced them?

Not that she wanted to put the younger doctor in a difficult position by asking him outright. It wouldn't be fair. Instead, she encouraged him to chatter on their way back to Resus. And then she didn't have time to think about Daniel Capaldi when the paramedics brought in a patient. Dev, the lead paramedic, did the handover.

'Mrs Jane Burroughes, aged sixty-seven, otherwise healthy until today when she slipped in the garden and banged her head on the rockery. She remembers blacking out but she was conscious when we arrived. We put a neck brace on and we think she's fractured her cheekbone and her arm. I'm not happy about her eye, either,' Dev said.

From the amount of blood on Jane Burroughes's cheek, it was entirely possible she'd damaged her eye and they'd need to bring in a specialist.

'Pain relief?' Beatrice asked.

'She refused it,' Dev said. 'I haven't put a line in.'

'Thank you,' she said.

She introduced herself and Josh to Mrs Burroughes. 'We'd like to make you a bit more comfortable while we check you over. I know you refused pain relief in the ambulance, but can I give you some pain relief now?'

'I don't like the way it makes me feel, woozy and sick,' Mrs Burroughes said.

'When I had my wisdom teeth out and they put stuff in my arm, I felt drunk for two days afterwards.'

'I could give you some paracetamol?' Beatrice suggested. 'That won't make you feel woozy, and it'll take the edge off the pain. It won't be as effective as a stronger painkiller, but you'll feel a little bit more comfortable.'

Finally Mrs Burroughes agreed to have paracetamol.

'We'll need to do a CT scan of her neck,' Beatrice said to Josh, 'and call the ophthalmology team for their view on Mrs Burroughes's eye.'

Thankfully the CT scan showed no problems with Mrs Burroughes's neck, so they were able to remove the neck brace; the ophthalmology team was able to confirm that the laceration was fixable and Mrs Burroughes wasn't going to lose her sight. Finally the X-ray showed that the break in Mrs Burroughes's arm was clean and could be treated with a cast rather than surgery.

Beatrice had just finished treating her patient and arranged a handover to the ward when Sam Price came in.

'Beatrice, it's lunchtime,' he said, 'and Hayley—my wife, who's coming back to work here part time next month—suggested meeting us in the canteen. Josh, are you coming with us?'

The younger doctor blushed. 'I…um…'

Sam raised an eyebrow. 'Got a date?'

Josh nodded, and Sam patted his shoulder. 'Just be yourself and don't worry. She'll adore you.'

Sam took Beatrice to the canteen. 'So how was your first morning?' he asked.

'Fine.' Apart from Daniel Capaldi. Not that she was going to let herself think about him. 'Josh is a sweetie.'

'He's a nice lad. Though I feel a bit guilty because—well, I assume you must've heard about the staff day out I organised?' Sam asked.

'Go-karting on ice, you mean?'

'It's great fun,' he said with a grin. 'But I'm a reformed character now. No bungee-jumping, no go-karting on ice and no abseiling—well, unless it's for work.'

'Abseiling at work?' Beatrice couldn't help laughing. 'I'm not sure that's part of the average Emergency Department's duties.'

He laughed back. 'It can be, if it's a MERIT team job, but don't tell Haze because she worries.'

'Got you.'

Hayley Price was waiting for them at the entrance to the canteen. Sam greeted her with a kiss. 'Beatrice, this is Hayley; Hayley, Beatrice.' He smiled. 'And this gorgeous little bundle is Darcie.' He scooped the baby out of the lightweight pram, and the baby cooed at him and pulled his hair.

'Lovely to meet you, Beatrice, and welcome to Muswell Hill Memorial Hospital,' Hayley said. 'So how has your first day in the department been?'

'Great. Everyone's been lovely.' Almost everyone. She wasn't going to make a fuss.

'They're a good bunch,' Hayley said.

'She's a good one, too,' Sam said. 'Our kitchen's full of the best brownies I've ever tasted. Did you spend all last night baking them, Beatrice?'

She smiled. 'No, and I had a bit of help. Make sure you grab one for Hayley.'

By the time they'd bought their lunch and settled at a table, still chatting, Beatrice was feeling very much part of the team.

'So you're coming back part time next month?' she asked Hayley.

Hayley nodded. 'Much as I love my daughter, I miss work. Part time seemed like a good compromise.'

'I agree,' Beatrice said.

'If you'd like a cuddle with Darcie, better get it in now because the whole department will swoop on her when we walk in,' Sam said.

A cuddle with the baby.

Beatrice thought of her own baby, the stillborn daughter she'd held for a few brief minutes. What if that car hadn't crashed into her? What if she hadn't had the abruption, and Taylor had been born around her due date, alive?

But now wasn't the time or place to think about it. None of that was Sam's or Hayley's fault. She forced herself to smile brightly and scooped the baby from Sam's arms. 'She's gorgeous.'

'You're good with babies,' Hayley said when Darcie promptly yawned and fell asleep.

Again, Beatrice shut the door in her head. 'It comes from having three nephews and a niece. The youngest one's four now.' And how hard it had been to hold him. 'But I'm an old hand at getting them to go to sleep.'

'I'll remember that and get you to teach

me some tricks when Madam here starts teething,' Hayley said. 'Right. So, tell us all about you. Where did you train, where were you before here, do you have a partner and children…?'

'Haze, give the poor woman a chance to breathe!' Sam admonished, though he was smiling and looked as if he wanted to know the answers, too.

'It's fine. I trained at the Hampstead Free and I worked there until I came here,' Beatrice said with a smile. The next bit was more tricky. Telling the whole truth would mean that her new colleagues would pity her as much as they had at the Hampstead Free, and she really didn't want that. Better to keep it simple and stick to the bare bones. The facts, and no explanations. 'No partner, no children.' To make sure nobody would try any well-meaning matchmaking, she added, 'And I'm concentrating very happily on my career.' And now it was time to change the subject. 'Can I ask you something confidential? I know I probably could've asked Josh, but I didn't want to put him in an awkward position.'

'Sure. Ask away,' Hayley said.

'It's about Daniel Capaldi,' Beatrice said.

Sam and Hayley exchanged a glance, looking slightly uneasy.

'I knew there was something. What am I missing?' Beatrice asked.

'Daniel's a nice guy,' Sam said carefully.

What he wasn't saying was obvious. Beatrice wasn't afraid to put it into words. 'But?'

Hayley blew out a breath. 'There isn't a tactful way to say it, but I get the impression you're a straight-talker so I know you won't take this the wrong way. Everyone thought his name was on the consultant's job.'

'So I've got his job and he resents me for it.'

'Not *necessarily*,' Sam said.

'But probably. Anyone would feel that way, in his shoes.' Beatrice bit her lip. 'OK. Thanks for the warning. I'll be careful what I say to him. I don't want to rub it in and make him feel bad.'

'At the end of the day, the management team chose you,' Hayley said. 'He'll get over it.'

At least now Beatrice understood why Daniel had been a little snippy with her and less welcoming than other members of the team. She'd be careful with him—not patronising, but not throwing her weight around, either.

After Hayley scooped the sleeping baby out of Beatrice's arms and transferred her to the pram, Beatrice enjoyed having lunch with them. Muswell Hill was a good place. She had the strongest feeling that she was going to be happy here.

'It's not just about work, though,' Hayley said. 'There's the regular pub quiz between us, Maternity and Paediatrics. How's your general knowledge?'

Beatrice thought of her brothers. 'A bit obscure.'

'Good. You're on the team,' Sam said. 'There's a team ten-pin bowling night in a couple of weeks—everything's on the noticeboard in the staff kitchen, if you want to sign up. Oh, and we're having a football morning in the park on Saturday. It's not a serious thing, really just the chance for everyone to kick a ball around, but we do a pot-luck picnic thing afterwards. And, after trying your brownies this morning…'

Beatrice smiled. 'Hint taken. OK. I don't mind kicking a ball about. And I'll make some more brownies.'

'Excellent. I think you're going to fit right in,' Sam said with a smile.

'Josh said the Red Lion's the place to go, so I'm buying drinks after my shift today,' Beatrice said. 'If you can both make it, it'd be lovely to see you.'

'That's nice of you,' Hayley said. 'Thanks. We'll be there.'

Back in the staff kitchen, as Sam had predicted, everyone wanted to cuddle baby Darcie. And people Beatrice hadn't yet met patted her on the shoulder, welcomed her to the department, and thanked her for the brownies.

Daniel Capaldi was conspicuously absent; and Beatrice noticed that he didn't come to the Red Lion with the rest of the team after their shift. She could understand that. If you were really disappointed at not getting a promotion everyone thought you'd earned, it would be hard to celebrate someone else getting the post instead.

But there was a strong chance she and Daniel would have to work together in the future, and she needed to be sure that they could do that and put the needs of their patients before any professional rivalry. As the more senior of them, it was up to her to sort it out.

There were two ways she could deal with this. She could either pretend it wasn't happening and wait for Daniel to stop resenting her; or she could tackle the problem head on and come to some kind of understanding with him. She'd grown up with their family motto, *tenacitas per aspera*—strength through adversity—so the second option was the one the rest of the Lindfords would choose.

Tackling him head on it was.

The next day, she was in Cubicles and Daniel was in Resus. Just as Sam had done, the previous day, she slipped into Resus at lunchtime. Daniel was on his own, to her relief, and it looked as if he was writing up notes. 'Dr Capaldi. Just the man I wanted to see,' she said.

He gave her a cool look. 'Something I can help you with, Ms Lindford?'

'Yes. I'm buying you lunch.'

'Thank you, but that's not necessary.'

He was trying to fob her off? Well, she wasn't put off that easily. 'I rather think it is. You and I need a chat.'

'Hardly.'

'Definitely,' she said. 'I'm not pulling rank, but I think there's a problem and we need to sort it out rather than let it grow out of proportion.'

'There isn't a problem,' he said.

'Then have lunch with me.'

He looked reluctant.

'Don't worry, I'm not going to put arsenic in your coffee,' she said. 'Apart from anything else, I don't have the licence to get hold of that grade of poison.'

He didn't even crack a smile.

Taking him by the shoulders and shaking him until his teeth rattled wouldn't achieve anything other than a temporary relief from frustration. She folded her arms to help her resist the temptation. 'I could offer you a pair of boxing gloves, if that would make you feel better. Though I should probably make you aware that I could take you in the gym.'

He blinked. 'You box?'

'I box,' she confirmed. Her personal trainer had suggested it, and boxing had been one of the things that had got her on the slow road back from rock bottom. 'I might be a galumphing five foot ten, but I'm very light on my feet. I can do the whole Muhammed Ali thing. So. Your choice. Boxing gloves or lunch?'

'Lunch. Because I'd never hit a woman.'

'I wouldn't have any qualms about hitting *you* in the ring,' she said.

Was that a fleeting and grudging glimpse of respect she saw in his face?

'But I think coffee night be more civilised,' she said.

He didn't make polite conversation on the way to the canteen, but neither did she. And although Daniel protested when she insisted on paying for his sandwiches, Beatrice gave him the look she reserved for patients who were drunk and obnoxious on a Saturday night and he backed off.

'Thank you for lunch,' he muttered when they sat down.

At least he had manners. Even if he wouldn't look her in the eye. And that was going to change, too. She'd make him smile at her if it killed her.

'Let's put our cards on the table. I understand why you don't like me. I got the job that everyone thought had your name written all over it. Of course you resent me.'

'Not true,' he said.

She scoffed. 'You were the only person who didn't take a brownie yesterday.'

'Because I don't like chocolate.'

That hadn't occurred to her. But she hadn't finished with her evidence. 'And you didn't come to my welcome drink after your shift.'

'And you think that was because I'm sulking?'

'Isn't it?'

'No,' he said. 'Everyone else thought my name was on that job. That's the only bit you got right.'

She frowned. 'So what's your take on it?'

'Not that it's anybody's business, but I didn't actually apply for the job.'

She stared at him. 'You didn't?'

'I didn't,' he confirmed. 'Because I can't give the department what it needs, right now. I'm a single dad, and my son's needs come before the job. Always.'

She blew out a breath. 'Fair enough. I didn't know that.'

'Well, you do now.'

'Then I apologise for jumping to conclusions.'

* * *

Daniel hadn't expected her to react quite like that. He'd expected her to go haughty on him, as she had the previous day.

And he hadn't exactly been fair to her. He could've told her that he wasn't going to her welcome drinks, and why. Instead, he'd chickened out and just avoided her.

He needed to put that right. 'And I'm sorry for letting you think I resent you for taking my job.'

'OK. So we're saying now that the problem between us isn't a problem.'

Oh, there was a problem, all right. His libido was practically sitting up and begging. But he was just going to have to ignore it. 'There isn't a problem,' he lied. 'Welcome to Muswell Hill.'

'Thank you.'

'And you didn't have to buy me lunch.'

'Call it in lieu of the drink you didn't have last night,' she said.

He inclined his head. 'Then thank you.' Polite, he could do.

'So how old is your son?' she asked.

'Four.' Was it his imagination, or did she just flinch?

Imagination, maybe, because then she smiled. 'It's a lovely age. My youngest nephew is four.'

She had a killer smile. If Daniel hadn't known it was anatomically impossible, he would've said that his heart had just done a backflip. But, for Iain's sake, he couldn't act on the attraction he felt towards Beatrice Lindford. It wouldn't be fair to bring someone else into the little boy's life—someone who might not stick around. Someone who was, to all intents and purposes, his boss. It would be too complicated. Inappropriate. 'Uh-huh,' he said, not sure quite what to say to her. How to stop this from tipping over into personal stuff he didn't want to share. Such as why he was a single dad.

'Stating the obvious, but from your accent it sounds as if you're from Scotland.'

'Glasgow,' he confirmed.

'With an Italian surname?'

'My great-grandparents were Italian.' He paused. 'And you're posh.'

'Yes. But I'm a girl and I'm the youngest, so I got to choose what I wanted to do.'

Meaning that her brother—or brothers— had been expected to go into the family business? But asking her would be too personal;

and it would also mean she could ask him
personal stuff that he didn't want to answer.
He backed off. 'So you trained as a doctor.'

'Here in London. What about you? Glasgow or here?'

'Here,' he said. And please don't let her
ask about his son.

'So what made you pick emergency medicine?' she asked.

Relief flooded through him. He could talk
about work and why he did what he did. It
wasn't quite so personal, so it was easier
to deal with. 'I like the fact that we make a
real difference, that we can save people.' He
paused. 'You?'

'Pretty much the same. Though we can't
save everyone.'

Again, there was an odd look on her
face—as if she was talking about some-
thing personal. But he wasn't going to ask.
It was none of his business. Instead, he said,
'We do our best. That's all any of us can do.
Strive to do our best.'

'True.'

He finished his coffee. 'Thank you for
lunch. And for the chat.'

'So we're good?'

'It won't be a problem working together,

if that's what you mean.' He'd already heard Josh singing her praises, saying that Beatrice was good with patients and she listened to the rest of the team. That was good. He hated it when senior colleagues went all arrogant. It was never good for the patients.

'I'm glad. We don't have to be friends,' she said. 'As long as we agree that our patients come first.'

'That works for me,' he said. 'We'd better get back to the ward.'

'OK.' She swallowed the last of her own coffee. 'Let's go.'

CHAPTER TWO

THE REST OF the week went smoothly; Beatrice still wasn't rostered in the same part of the department as Daniel during their shifts, but at least he was civil to her if they happened to be in the staff kitchen at the same time.

On Saturday morning, she headed to the park for the team's football day out. As Sam had requested, she made some brownies. Remembering that Daniel didn't like chocolate, she also made flapjacks, as a kind of peace offering. Then again, Daniel might not be there.

She'd just added her offerings to the picnic table when Daniel turned up with a small boy in tow. Even if she hadn't known that he had a four-year-old son, she would've known that the little boy was Daniel's because they looked so alike. And she was faintly amused to discover that the little boy had a Glaswegian accent almost as strong as his father's.

But what she hadn't expected was that Daniel would look so gorgeous in a football kit. The tight-fitting T-shirt showed that he had good abs, and his legs were strong and muscular. He looked more like a model than a doctor, and she wasn't surprised to see how many admiring glances were headed his way.

'I didn't think you'd be here today,' Daniel said. 'Or are you a football fan as well as a boxing fan?'

She pushed away the thought of getting hot and sweaty in a boxing ring with him. That really wasn't appropriate. 'Hayley and Sam said everyone turns up and has a huge picnic afterwards. I thought it might be a nice way to get to know the team outside work,' she said.

Daniel shrugged. 'Fair enough.'

'Do you work with my daddy?' the little boy asked.

'I do,' Beatrice confirmed.

He looked at her. 'You're *really* tall for a girl.'

'Iain, don't be rude,' Daniel began.

'It's fine, and he's right—I *am* tall.' She

smiled, and crouched down so she was nearer to the little boy's height. 'Is that better?'

'Yes,' he said. 'Hello. I'm Iain.'

'I'm Beatrice.' She held out her hand for him to shake.

He shook her hand, but frowned. 'That's a strange name.'

'You can call me Bea, for short.'

He wrinkled his nose. 'Like a buzzy bee?'

She couldn't resist Iain's charm and chutzpah. 'Just like that,' she said.

'Hello, Bee. Are you going to play football?'

'No, I'm just going to watch,' she said.

'I play football. Just like my dad,' Iain told her proudly, puffing out his chest.

'Then I'll make sure I cheer really loudly when you score a goal,' she said.

Although football really wasn't her thing, she enjoyed chatting to Hayley on the sidelines, and dutifully clapped and cheered every time a goal was scored.

Iain was running past her, clearly intent on getting to the ball, when he tripped and fell over. Instinctively, she looked up to see where Daniel was: on the far side of the field.

Iain was on his knees, crying and shielding his arm.

What could she do but go over to him until his dad arrived and see if she could sort out the problem?

'You're lucky we're all in the emergency department so we know just how to deal with things when people fall over,' she said. 'Where does it hurt, Iain?'

'Here.' He pointed to his elbow.

It was very obvious to her that he'd twisted his arm when he fell, so the ligament holding the radial bone in place had slipped, letting the bone dislocate. Given that he was so young, it would be easy to manipulate the bone back into place—but she also knew that it would hurt like mad, very briefly.

'I need you to be super-brave for me, Iain,' she said. 'Do you like chocolate?'

'Aye.'

'OK. I can fix what's wrong, but it means I have to touch your poorly arm and it'll hurt for about three seconds. After that, it'll stop hurting,' she said. 'I made some really special chocolate brownies you might like, so you can have one afterwards. I just need you to be brave for three seconds, that's all. Can you do that for me?'

Iain sobbed, 'I want my dad.'

'And he's running across the field towards

you right now. He'll be here really soon. But I really need to slip that bone back into place for you,' she said. 'Close your eyes and sing me a song, Iain.'

'I don't know any songs,' he wailed, clearly too scared to be able to think.

'I bet you know "The Wheels on the Bus",' she said. 'I'll help you sing it. And I want you to sing it really, really loudly. Can you do that?'

He nodded, his face wet with tears.

She started singing, and the little boy closed his eyes and began to sing along with her, very loudly and very out of tune. The perfect distraction, she hoped. One quick movement and she'd manipulated his arm to put the bone back into place.

Iain was halfway through yelling when he clearly realised that his arm had stopped hurting.

'Oh. It doesn't hurt any more,' he said. 'You fixed me!'

'I did,' she said with a smile.

Daniel arrived just as Iain flung his arms around Beatrice and hugged her. 'Thank you, Bee!'

'What happened?' he asked.

'He fell over and dislocated his elbow. I've just manipulated it back, but we need to check his pulses and his range of movement.' Just in case there was a problem and Iain needed an X-ray, Daniel knew.

His own heart was racing madly with fear for his child, but she'd been calm and sorted out the problem without any fuss. He'd do the same. It was what he'd trained all these years for: to be calm when there was an accident or an emergency.

'Iain, can you move your arms for me and copy what I do?' he asked.

'Aye, Dad.'

He checked Iain's pulses, which were fine, then talked Iain through a range of movements. The little boy copied every movement without flinching or stopping as if he was in pain. Everything seemed completely normal.

'I hardly need to tell you what happens next,' Beatrice said.

'Pain relief if he needs it, put him in a sling for the rest of today to support his elbow, and if he stiffens up and doesn't use his arm tomorrow take him in for an X-ray.'

She spread her hands. 'Textbook perfect, Dr Capaldi.'

'Thank you for looking after him,' he said.

'That's what I'm here for. That,' she said, 'and chocolate brownies. I haven't forgotten what I promised you, Iain.'

'My dad doesn't like chocolate. We never have chocolate brownies,' Iain said.

'Then your dad can go and finish playing football while you sit and eat brownies with me,' she said.

'I…' Daniel looked at her, wanting to be with his son but not wanting to let the rest of the team down, either.

Beatrice shooed him back to the field. 'He'll be fine with me.' And then she gave him the sassiest smile he'd ever seen, one that made him want to grab her and kiss her. Not good.

'Trust me—I'm a doctor,' she said.

It was the cheesiest line in the book. But he'd seen her at work and he'd heard others praising her, saying that she always put the patient first. And Iain seemed to like her. He gave her a speaking look, but headed back to the field. He played for another ten minutes, and then to his relief he was substituted by one of the nurses.

When he went back over to where the spectators were, Iain was chatting animatedly to Beatrice. And Beatrice had used the scarf from her hair to fashion into a sling.

'Dad! You're back!'

'That's my playing over for today,' he said. 'Thank you for looking after Iain. I'll take over now.'

'My pleasure. We've had a nice time, haven't we, Iain?' she asked.

'She made me a special sling,' Iain said. 'Look.'

'Very nice,' Daniel said. 'I'll wash it when we get home and get it back to you on Monday at work. And now we must let Ms Lindford get on, Iain.'

The little boy frowned. 'But I like talking to Bee.'

'She's busy.'

Out of Iain's view, she shook her head.

She wasn't undermining him as a parent— he appreciated the fact she'd disagreed with him without actually saying so in front of his son—but the idea of spending time with her was dangerous. Right now Beatrice's hair was loose, she was wearing denims cut off at the knee, a strappy top and canvas shoes; and she looked more approachable than she did at work in tailored trousers and a white coat. The way she looked right now, he could just imagine walking hand in hand with her in the sunshine and kissing her under a tree.

He didn't want to walk hand in hand with anyone in the sunshine or kiss them under a tree, and that included Beatrice Lindford, he told himself sharply.

'Five more minutes, Dad?' Iain pleaded. 'Please.'

Again, out of Iain's view, she nodded.

Iain's brown eyes were huge and pleading. How could he resist? 'All right. Five more minutes.'

'Bee makes the best chocolate brownies in the world,' Iain said. 'Even you would like them, Dad.'

'I made flapjacks as well.' She gave him a cheeky grin. 'And don't tell me that you don't like oats. You're a Scot.'

'Aye, he is.' Iain was all puffed up with pride. 'And so am I.'

'Peas in a pod, you two.'

But Daniel could see she was laughing with them, not at them.

'Can I have some flapjacks, too, Bee?' Iain asked.

'That's your dad's call, not mine,' she said, lifting her hands in a gesture of surrender.

'Yes,' Daniel said. 'Though there's a word missing, Iain Capaldi.'

'Please,' Iain said.

Daniel ended up trying a flapjack himself, and it surprised him. 'That's actually better than my grandmother's—and don't you dare tell your great-gran I said that, Iain,' he added swiftly.

'My great-granny makes the best ice cream in the world,' Iain said. 'Do you like ice cream, Bee?'

'I do,' Beatrice said with a smile, completely charmed by the way he pronounced his Rs.

'You should come to Glasgow and try my great-granny's special ice cream. It's fab.'

'Maybe sometime,' Beatrice said.

Iain chattered away to her, and Daniel couldn't help watching them. Iain was usually shy with strangers, so it was unusual for him to be so talkative. Maybe it was because Beatrice had reduced his dislocated elbow and stopped him being in such pain. Or maybe he was responding to her gentleness.

Against his better judgement, he was starting to like Beatrice Lindford. Too much for his own peace of mind. She was the first woman since Jenny he'd even thought about holding hands with, let alone anything else. Which made her dangerous.

Iain didn't stop talking about her all the way home, either.

'She looks like a princess,' he said. 'She's got real golden hair.'

Hair that Daniel couldn't get out of his head, now he'd seen it loose.

'And it's long.'

Yeah. Daniel had noticed.

'Like the princess in the story Miss Shields told us in class. The one in the tower. Her hair was so long she could make it into a ladder. Ra…' He paused, his forehead wrinkled in a frown as he tried to remember the princess's name.

'Rapunzel,' Daniel supplied.

'Aye. And she talks like the Queen, all posh.'

'Yes.'

'I like her. Do you like her, Dad?'

Awkward question. 'I work with her,' Daniel prevaricated.

'She's nice. Can she come for tea tonight?'

'No, Iain. She's busy.'

But his son wasn't to be put off. 'Next week, then?'

'She might be busy.'

'Ask her,' Iain said. 'Go on, Dad. Ask her. Please.'

'Do you want to go and get pizza?' Daniel asked, hoping to distract his son with a treat.

It worked. Until bedtime, when Iain started on about princesses again. 'Do you think Bee's married to a prince?'

Daniel had no idea, but maybe if Iain thought Beatrice was married he'd drop the subject. 'Probably.'

'Then why didn't the prince come to play football today?'

Daniel loved his son dearly, but the constant questions could be exhausting. 'Maybe he can't play football.'

'Oh.' Iain paused. 'If she's a princess, do you think she knows the Queen?'

'I don't know, Iain.'

'Mum likes Prince Harry.'

Daniel tamped down his irritation. 'I know.'

'Do you think Bee knows Prince Harry?'

'I think,' Daniel said gently, 'it's time for one more story and then sleep.'

He just hoped his son wouldn't say anything about Beatrice next weekend, when Iain was due to stay with his mother. The last thing he wanted was Jenny quizzing him about whether he was dating again. He knew she still felt guilty about what had happened between them, and that if he started seeing someone it would make her feel better, but he really didn't want to date anyone. He wanted to concentrate on bringing Iain up and being the best dad he could be.

On Sunday, Iain seemed to have forgotten about his new friend. But then on Monday Daniel picked up his son from nursery, and Iain handed him a picture: a drawing of a woman with long golden hair and a crown, a man playing football and a small boy with red lines coming out of his elbow.

'It's Bee making me better on Saturday,' he announced, although Daniel had already worked that out for himself. 'I drawed it for her. Can you give it to her tomorrow?'

'All right.'

Iain beamed. 'I know she'll like it.'

'I'm sure she will.' If she didn't, he'd fib and tell Iain that she loved it. No way was he going to let his little boy be disappointed.

Beatrice was in the staff kitchen when he walked in, the next day. 'Are you busy at lunchtime?' he asked.

She looked surprised, then answered carefully. 'It depends what it's like in Resus.'

'OK. If you're not busy, I need to talk to you—and lunch is on me.'

She shook her head. 'There's no need.'

'I want to say thank you for rescuing Iain on Saturday. His arm's fine, by the way.'

'Good, but really there's no need to buy me lunch. I just did what anyone else would've done because I was the nearest one to him when it happened. Though thank you for the offer.'

'Can I just talk to you, then?' He really didn't want to give her the picture in front of everyone.

She nodded. 'We'll go halves on lunch.'

'Good.'

Daniel switched into work mode, and managed to concentrate on his patients for the morning: two fractures, a badly sprained ankle and an elderly woman who'd had a TIA and whom he admitted for further testing. He had no idea how busy Resus had been, but at lunchtime Beatrice appeared. 'Are you OK to go, or do you need a bit of time to finish writing up notes?'

'I'm OK to go,' he said.

He waited until they were sitting in the canteen before handing her the envelope.

'What's this?' she asked.

'Iain asked me to give you this,' he said.

She opened the envelope, looked at the picture and smiled. Her blue eyes were full of warmth when she looked at him. 'That's lovely—me, him and you at the team football day on Saturday, I'm guessing?'

He nodded.

'Tell him thank you, I love it, and I'm going to put it on my fridge, right next to the picture Persephone drew me of her horse at the weekend.'

'Persephone?' Daniel asked.

'My niece.'

He blinked. 'So your family goes in for unusual names.'

She nodded. 'My generation's all from Shakespeare—Orlando's the oldest, then Lysander, then me.' She spread her hands. 'It could've been worse. My mother could've called me Desdemona or Goneril. And, actually, Beatrice is Shakespeare's best female character, so I'm quite happy to be named after her.'

Her accent alone marked her out as posh. The names of her brothers and her niece marked her out as seriously posh. And had she just said that her niece had a horse? Posh *and* rich, then.

Then he realised what he'd said. 'I didn't mean to be rude about your name. We just have…simpler names in my family.'

'Then you'd approve of Sandy's choices—George and Henry.'

'Sandy?'

'Lysander.' She smiled. 'Mummy's the only one who's allowed to call him that. Anyone else gets his evil glare and never dares do it again.'

'So Persephone is your oldest brother's daughter, then?'

She nodded. 'We call her Seffy, for short. And her older brother is Odysseus.'

'Odysseus.' Who wouldn't have lasted three seconds in the playground at Daniel's school. Why on earth would you call a child Odysseus?

As if the question was written all over his face, Beatrice explained, 'Orlando studied classics. So did his wife. They wanted to use names from Greek mythology for their children—and their dogs.' She grinned. 'They have a black Lab called Cerberus—although he only has one head, he barks enough for three and it drives Mummy crackers.'

She called her mother 'Mummy'? Posher still. Beatrice Lindford was way, way out of his league.

Not that he was thinking of asking her out.

The attraction he felt towards her needed to be stifled. The sooner, the better.

She looked at the drawing again. 'Why am I wearing a crown?'

'Iain says you talk like the Queen and you've got hair like a princess, so he's decided you must be a princess and therefore you also know the Queen and Prince Harry.'

She laughed. 'That's cute.'

'I tried to tell him you're not a princess.'

'Absolutely not.'

'Are you sure? Because… Well…'

'Because I have a posh accent and most of my family have unusual names? That's a bit of a sweeping generalisation. It'd be like me saying you're from Glasgow so everything you eat must be fried.'

'True, and I didn't mean to be rude.'

Beatrice definitely wasn't going to tell Daniel that she had grown up in a castle. Or that actually her father was a viscount, making her family minor royalty. He didn't need to know any of that. All he needed to know about her was that she was a doctor, and she was good at her job.

'Apology accepted. And I love Iain's drawing.' She smiled at him. 'He's a nice boy.'

'And he hasn't stopped talking about you, or asking when you can come to tea. I've told him you're busy and you're probably married to a prince.' Daniel rolled his eyes. 'That's what started all the Prince Harry stuff. His mum likes Prince Harry.'

So Daniel had clearly split up from his partner rather than being a widower. It was unusual for a dad to have custody of the child, but asking him about the situation felt like prying. 'Prince Harry is gorgeous,' she said. 'Your wife has good—' She stopped dead. Uh-oh. *Good taste.* That was tantamount to saying that she fancied Daniel.

Which she didn't.

Well, a little bit.

Well, quite a lot.

But things were complicated. She had the job he claimed he hadn't applied for but which everyone thought had had his name on it. He had a son who was clearly the focus of his life, and dating would be tricky for him. Plus she didn't want to tell him about her past and see the pity in his face.

Better to keep this professional.

'Good taste in princes,' she finished.

'I'll tell her that. Because Iain's going to tell her all about you when he sees her this weekend.' He sighed. 'You wouldn't believe how much a four-year-old boy can talk.'

Or girl. She thought of Taylor and her heart squeezed. Would her little girl have been a chatterbox?

Not here. Not now.

'Oh, I would. George could talk the hind leg off a donkey. He's four,' she said. A month younger than Taylor would've been. And how hard it had been to walk into her sister-in-law's hospital room and hold that baby in her arms for the first time. She'd had to force herself to smile and hold back the tears. 'George is the youngest of my nephews, and his big thing is dinosaurs. You wouldn't believe how many complicated names he can pronounce. Give him a bucket of wooden bricks and he'll build you a stegosaurus in two minutes flat.'

'Iain loves dinosaurs, too. And rockets. My mum painted a mural in his bedroom of dinosaurs in a rocket heading for the moon, and he loves it.'

'I bet.' She glanced at her watch, knowing that she was being a coward and cutting this short. But she couldn't afford to get emotionally involved with Daniel Capaldi and his son. 'Better get back to the ward. Please thank Iain for his drawing. It's lovely.'

'I will.' He looked relieved, as if she'd let him off the hook.

So did that mean he felt this ridiculous attraction, too?

Well, even if he did, they weren't going to act on it. They were going to be professional. Keep things strictly business between them. And that was that.

CHAPTER THREE

OVER THE NEXT couple of days, Daniel's determination to keep things strictly professional was sorely tested, particularly when he and Beatrice were rostered on together in Resus.

Their first patient of the day was Maureen Bishop, an elderly woman who'd slipped and fallen backwards off the patio, and was badly injured, enough for the air ambulance to bring her in.

'Thankfully her neighbour had arranged to pop round for a cup of tea, couldn't get an answer and went round the back of the house and found her,' the paramedic from the air ambulance explained. 'She was unconscious, so the neighbour called the ambulance—who called us to bring her in. She's come round now, but she's got a nasty gash in the back of her head from falling against a pot, plus fractured ribs, and we're a bit worried she might have a crack in her skull or a bleed in her brain.'

'Have you given her any pain relief?' Beatrice asked.

The paramedic nodded and gave her full details. 'We've put her on a spinal board with a neck brace.'

'Great. Has anyone managed to get in touch with her family?'

'Yes. Her daughter's on the way in.'

'That's good.' She went over to the trolley with Daniel. 'Hello, Mrs Bishop, I'm Beatrice and this is Daniel,' she said. 'We're looking after you today. May we call you Maureen?'

'Yes, love,' Maureen said.

'Can you remember what happened?'

The elderly woman grimaced. 'I slipped and fell.'

'Can you remember blacking out, or do you have any idea how long you were unconscious?' Beatrice asked.

'No,' Maureen whispered. 'I'm sorry.'

Beatrice squeezed her hand. 'No need to apologise. You've had a nasty fall. I'm going to send you for a scan because we need to check out that bump to your head, and also for X-rays so we can have a better look at your ribs, because we think you might have broken a few. Your daughter's on her way.'

'I didn't want to worry her. I told them not to call her at work,' Maureen said.

'If you were my mum,' Beatrice said gently, 'then I'd want to know you'd been taken to hospital. I'd be more upset if they didn't call me. And I'm betting it's just the same for your daughter.'

The CT scan showed a bleed to the brain; by the time Beatrice had liaised with the neurology team and persuaded them to admit Maureen, her daughter Jennifer had arrived.

'What happened?' Jennifer asked.

'Your mum slipped off the patio and banged her head against a pot. We know she was unconscious for a while, but not for how long. Fortunately her neighbour found her and called the ambulance,' Daniel explained.

'We sent your mum for a scan and X-rays,' Beatrice said. 'I'm pleased to say there's no evidence of any bones broken in her neck, so we can take the spinal collar off now, but she has fractured a couple of ribs, and when she hit her head it caused a bleed in her brain. She seems fine at the moment, but a bleed is a bit like a stroke in that sometimes it takes a few days for us to see what's happened. We're going to admit her to the neurology ward, so she's going to be monitored for the next day or so.'

'But she's going to be all right? She's not going to die?'

'She's holding her own at the moment,' Beatrice said, taking Jennifer's hand and squeezing it, 'but we want to keep an eye on her in case that bang on the head causes a problem. She'll be in good hands and we can treat her straight away if anything happens.' She smiled at Jennifer. 'Your mum was a bit worried about the paramedics calling you at work.'

'I got someone to cover my class,' Jennifer said. 'I'd be more upset if they hadn't called me.'

'That's exactly what I told her,' Beatrice said. 'I'll take you through now. It's going to look a bit scary because your mum's on a spinal board with a neck collar on, but that's absolutely standard when someone's had a fall and we think there might be any damage to the back or the neck. I'll let you say hello to her, and then we'll take off the collar and make her a bit more comfortable before she goes up to the ward.'

It was the first time Daniel had worked with Beatrice, and he could see for himself why Josh had sung her praises. Beatrice was very clear when she was managing Resus; everyone knew what they needed to do, and she was completely approachable. Josh had said that one of the nurses hadn't quite understood her instructions, the other day, and Beatrice had taken the time afterwards to go through the case, explaining exactly why she'd made certain decisions. And he really liked the way she was calm and kind to their patients.

The more Daniel worked with her, the more he liked her.

And, worse still, the more attracted he was to her. He couldn't seem to get a grip and push the unwanted feelings aside. Instead, he found himself wondering how soft her hair would be against his skin, and how her arms would feel around him. How her mouth would feel against his own.

For pity's sake. He was thirty-four, not seventeen. He had responsibilities. He didn't have time for this. He couldn't keep wondering what it would be like to date Beatrice.

If he didn't manage to sort his head out, he thought grimly, he'd need to have a word with whoever was doing the roster next month, to make sure he and Beatrice weren't working together.

Late on Thursday afternoon, Beatrice had to steel herself slightly when the paramedics brought in a woman who'd taken an overdose.

'I brought her in for the same thing, a month ago,' Dev, the lead paramedic, told Beatrice quietly. 'And another team brought her in a fortnight ago.'

'Three times in a month.' Beatrice frowned. 'I'll check her notes to see if anyone's referred her for counselling, but if they haven't then I definitely want to bring the psych team in. She needs help with the root cause. We can't just patch her up and send her home so she takes another overdose and comes back in again. That isn't fair to anyone.'

Dev spread his hands. 'Mental health. You know the situation there as well as I do.'

'Overstretched. I know.' Beatrice sighed.

'But I'll push as much as I can for her. Thanks for your help, Dev.'

She went over to the bed. 'I'm Beatrice, and I'm part of the team looking after you today,' she said to her patient. 'May I call you Sally?'

The young woman nodded.

'The paramedics tell me you took an overdose of paracetamol.'

Sally hunched her shoulders, and Beatrice sat down and took her hand. 'I'm not here to judge you, Sally, I'm here to help you. But I do need to know how many tablets you took, when, and over how long a period, so I know the best way to look after you.'

'A dozen tablets,' Sally whispered. 'An hour ago.'

'What did you take them with?' Beatrice asked, really hoping that alcohol wasn't involved.

'Water.'

That was one good thing; she didn't have to worry about complications from alcohol. 'OK. Normally paracetamol's safe to take as a painkiller, but if you take too much you can risk damaging your liver and your kidneys. I need to take some blood tests, and the results will tell me what the best treatment is for you. Is that OK?'

Sally nodded, and Beatrice took the bloods. 'Can I get you a cup of tea or something while we're waiting for the results?'

Sally shook her head. 'I'm all right.'

'I'll need to see some other patients while I'm waiting for the results, but I'll be back very soon to see you,' Beatrice said. 'If you're worried about anything, just press this buzzer to call one of us and we'll come in to see you, OK?'

Sally didn't ask for help while Beatrice called the psych team and asked for an urgent referral, or while Beatrice checked a set of X-rays for Josh and dealt with a nasty gash on an elderly man's arm where he'd slipped and knocked against a gatepost. But finally the blood test results came back, and Beatrice went into the cubicle where Sally was waiting quietly. The poor woman looked as if a huge weight was about to drop on her.

'I've got the test results back,' Beatrice said. 'We do need to treat you, to stop any damage happening to your liver, so I'm going to give you a drug through a drip— that's a line that goes straight into your vein. It means you'll need to stay with us another day while we give you the drug. Is that OK with you?'

Sally looked worried again. 'I felt so bad, last time. I was sick everywhere.'

'This is a different drug from the one you had last time. It's a special trial, but I used it in my last hospital and it's really good,' Beatrice said. 'It means you're less likely to have side effects, like being sick or itching. Tomorrow we'll do another blood test to see how you're doing, and we'll be able to let you go home if we're happy that there's no damage to your liver.'

Sally bit her lip. 'I'm so sorry.'

Beatrice squeezed her hand. 'You really don't have to apologise. You're not well and it's my job to make you better.'

'I know you're all busy here and you should be saving lives that matter, not bothering with me.'

'We are saving a life—*yours*,' Beatrice said gently. 'You're important, too.'

'I know I shouldn't have done it.'

'We all make mistakes.' And Beatrice had made this particular one herself. She could still remember how low she'd felt when she'd opened the box of paracetamol and popped the tablets out of their foil packaging. How hopeless.

'It seemed like the only way out.'

Just as it had for Beatrice. 'There's always another way,' she said, squeezing Sally's hand again. 'Though sometimes you need someone else to help you see it. Is there any-one we can call for you to let them know you're here? Your family, a friend?'

'Nobody.'

Beatrice remembered that feeling, too. Once she was out of Resus and in cubicles, she hadn't wanted the emergency staff to call her husband or her family, because she knew they'd blame themselves for not pick-ing up on the signs. And she hadn't wanted to burden any of her friends with how low she was feeling. She'd just been grateful that she hadn't been treated in her own depart-ment so she hadn't had the sheer embarrass-ment of having to face them all afterwards.

'I just don't want to be here,' Sally said, her voice shaking.

'I know, sweetheart, but I really can't let you go until you're better,' Beatrice said, still holding her hand. 'I need to be sure you're not going to collapse with liver damage.'

'It's wrong to be here.' Sally dragged in a breath. 'I just wish I was dead.'

Beatrice had once been in Sally's shoes, wanting to be with her lost baby instead of stuck here in this world. 'I promise, there's light at the end of the tunnel. We'll help you find it,' she said gently.

The psych team had sent a message to say that nobody was going to be available for another hour. Maybe there was something she could do for Sally until they got here, Beatrice thought. The same thing that the psych team at a different hospital had done for her, all those years ago: a grounding exercise she still used from time to time, when things got on top of her.

'I want you to do something for me, Sally,' she said. 'It might sound a bit weird, but humour me.'

'What's that?' Sally asked.

'I want you to tell me five things you can see.'

Sally blinked and frowned. 'Um—you, the curtain, the bed, I don't know the name of the machine over there, and a cup of water.' She ticked the items off on her fingers.

'That's great. Now four things you can

hear. It doesn't have to be here or right now in the hospital, just four sounds.'

'Waves on a beach, a machine beeping…' Sally paused. 'A bird singing, a child laughing.'

'That's great.' Especially because she'd named something positive. 'Now I want you to name three things you can touch—and touch them.'

'The sheet, a cup, the bed frame.' Sally touched them as she named them.

'That's really good. Two things you like the smell of?'

'Coffee and fresh bread.' Sally sounded more confident now.

'Brilliant. And now I want you to take one slow, deep breath. In for three—and now out for three.'

Sally did the deep breath while Beatrice counted, then looked at her. 'I don't know what you just did, but I don't feel as panicky as I did.'

'It's a grounding technique,' Beatrice explained. 'You can do it yourself any time you feel bad. It makes you focus on something external instead of your thoughts and feelings, and it stops the spiral of misery getting tighter. Five things you can see, four things you can hear, three things you can touch, two things you can smell, and one slow, deep breath.'

'What if I can't remember the order?' Sally asked.

'It doesn't matter. Just think of the five senses, pick one and start with that,' Beatrice said. 'Count down each time, and just remember that one breath at the end.'

Sally's eyes filled with tears. 'Thank you.'

'That's what I'm here for. To help,' Beatrice reassured her.

Although it was time for Beatrice's break, no way was she leaving her patient. She remembered what it was like to feel that you had nobody to understand or rely on. She sat with Sally until one of the nurses came in to say that the psych team had arrived, then headed out of the cubicle briefly to have a word with her colleague first.

'Keith Bradley from the psych team,' he said, introducing himself. 'Apparently you wanted a quick word?'

'Beatrice Lindford.' She shook his hand. 'It's my patient, Sally. I'm treating her for her third overdose in a month. I know resources are stretched,' she said, 'but this is just a revolving door and we're not helping her. We're just providing a sticking plaster and that's not good enough. We need to find the root cause of why she keeps taking an overdose and help her sort that out. Can you get her referred to emergency counselling?'

'It's like you said—resources are stretched —but I'll do what I can,' Keith said.

She rested her hand on his shoulder. 'Thanks. I appreciate it. I've done a grounding exercise with her, which has helped a bit, but she definitely needs you right now.'

She went back in to the cubicle and introduced Keith to Sally. 'I'm going to leave you with Keith now, but I'll be back to see you later today and see how you're getting on.'

Sally was pale but still determined not to call anyone when Beatrice dropped in to see her at the end of her shift.

'Keith was nice. And I did that thing you taught me when I felt bad after he'd gone, and it helped,' Sally said. 'Thank you.'

'I'm glad it helped. Are you sure I can't call anyone for you?'

'I'm sure. Right now I just can't face anyone,' Sally said.

But a good night's sleep had clearly made her feel differently, because in the morning when Beatrice came in with the blood test results Sally agreed to let the team call her mother.

'I'm happy to let you go home,' Beatrice said, 'but if you get a stomach ache or a really bad headache, you feel sick or drowsy, the whites of your eyes go yellow or you can't have a wee within the next eight hours, I want you to come back. I know that's a lot to remember, so I have a leaflet with all the information on that you can take home with you.'

'Thank you,' Sally said.

When Sally's mother came into the department, Beatrice had a quiet word with her in one of the cubicles.

'Keep an eye on her for the next twenty-four hours,' she said. 'I've given her a leaflet with symptoms to watch out for, following the treatment we gave her, and I can let you have a copy of that as well. We've got her referred to a counsellor, too, which should help.'

Sally's mother folded her arms; her mouth was set in a thin line. 'I can't believe Sally's done this yet again. This is the *third* time in a month. She's so selfish—she doesn't think about how it feels to get that call from the police or the hospital, or how hard it is to get time off work at the last minute to pick her up from here and look after her because she can't be left on her own.'

'I understand that it's hard for you, and it's worrying, too, but it's really not her fault,' Beatrice said. 'She's depressed to the point where she can't think clearly. She isn't doing it to cause problems for anyone else.' Her own family's stiff upper lip and refusal to talk about things had been tough enough to deal with, but overt hostility and anger like this… Poor Sally. Beatrice just hoped she had some good friends who would support her.

'I suppose so.' Sally's mother rolled her eyes. 'I'd better get her home. And let's hope she doesn't do it all over again next week.'

Daniel was in the cubicle next door and couldn't help overhearing the conversation.

Although he agreed with every word Beatrice had said, something about it felt personal. He was even more convinced during his break, when he'd boiled the kettle to make coffee and Beatrice walked into the kitchen, filled only half her mug with boiling water and then topped up her coffee with cold water so she could drink it straight down.

'Are you OK?' he asked.

She didn't meet his eyes and her voice was a little bit too bright when she replied, 'Yes, thanks, I'm fine.'

'I couldn't help overhearing you with the mum of your patient who'd taken an overdose. That sounded rough.'

Beatrice shrugged. 'I just hope she listened to me and realised that it's the illness at fault, not her daughter. Mental health's tricky to handle, and I know it's hard for the family to deal with.'

Mental health was very tricky; he knew that one first hand from Jenny's postnatal depression. Beatrice's words sounded personal, too. Had someone in her family or one of her friends suffered from depression? he wondered. Not that it was any of his business, and he wasn't going to pry. 'We do what we can,' he said.

'Yes.' She changed the subject. 'Are you going to the team ten-pin bowling thing tonight?'

'No. I'm looking after Iain,' he said. 'Are you going?'

'Yes. I'm rubbish at bowling, but it's fun—

and it's good to get to know people outside work.'

'Well, if I don't see you before the end of your shift, have fun,' he said lightly.

'Thanks. You have a good evening, too.'

Though Daniel had forgotten that he'd mentioned the team night out to his mother, who'd picked up Iain from school and given him his tea.

'I really think you should go on that team thing. It's Friday night. When did you last go out on a Friday night?' Susan asked.

Daniel couldn't actually remember, though he had a nasty feeling that his mother did.

'You're still young, Dan. You're thirty-four,' Susan said.

'And my focus is on bringing up my son.'

'Which is fine, but I'm not doing anything tonight so I can babysit for you. A night out with the team will do you good.'

'I don't need a night out, Mum, I'm fine.'

'It'll do you good,' Susan repeated. 'And Iain will be fine with me.'

'I know he will, but I can't ask you to give up your evening for me.'

'I've already told you I'm not busy, and you're not asking, I'm offering. And if you're worried about packing his stuff to go to Jenny's for the weekend, I can do that as well. It's no problem.' She rolled her eyes. 'Dan, I made enough mistakes when you were young. I let you down then. I want to be here for you now.'

'You have been there for me, Mum, when I needed you,' he reminded her. 'When it all went wrong with Jenny, I couldn't have coped without you. And I feel bad enough that you've relocated from Glasgow to London because of me and Iain.'

'You're my son. I love you dearly. Of course I was going to move to be with you and support you. But right now I want to shake you,' she added, folding her arms. 'Are you still in love with Jenny?'

'No.'

'Good, because she's married to someone else and she's not in love with you any more.'

He winced. 'Tell it to me straight, Mum, why don't you?'

'That's the only way to tell it,' she said. 'What you need is to move on and start dating someone.'

He thought of Beatrice, and quickly shoved the thought away. 'I don't need to date anyone.'

'Yes, you do, before you turn into a crabbit old man before your time.' She paused. 'What about Iain's Princess Bee?'

He shook his head. 'She's my colleague. Technically she might even be my boss. We can't date.'

Susan pounced. 'So you *have* thought about it, then.'

Several times. 'No,' he fibbed.

'Call her. Ask her if she's busy. Or maybe she'll be at the team thing tonight and you can see her there.'

Which was another reason why he shouldn't go. Spending time with her outside work could be dangerous for his peace of mind. 'Mum, I'm not looking for another relationship.'

'Iain's not going to be little for ever and ever. And I don't want you to be lonely when you're older.'

'You always tell me you're not lonely,' he pointed out.

'I'm not. I like my life. I go out with friends, I have a good time, and I enjoy working with my students.' She narrowed her eyes at him. 'You're going out tonight, Daniel Capaldi, whether you like it or not. And you're going to have a good time. Don't argue with your mother, because she knows much better than you do.'

He gave it one last shot. 'They had to book the places. They'll be full up.'

'There'll be room for you, even if you have to take turns bowling with someone.' She pursed her lips. 'It's a shame it's not tomorrow night, or you wouldn't have any excuses in the first place. But your excuses won't wash with me. You're going.'

And so he found himself going to the ten-pin bowling alley after he'd put Iain to bed and read him three stories.

'Daniel! So glad you're here—Kundini couldn't make it at the last minute and we were going to be one short,' Josh said. 'You're on Bea's team.'

Oh, help. She was the last person whose team he needed to be on. How was he possibly supposed to keep his distance?

It was made worse when he saw her; wearing jeans and a T-shirt, with her hair pulled back and tied by a scarf at the nape of her neck, she looked young and approachable—just as he imagined her to have looked in her student days. And right at that moment he wanted to walk up to her, wrap his arms round her and kiss her.

Which was the last thing he should do.

Instead, he walked up to her and said, 'I believe I'm your team's new substitute.'

The warmth of her smile almost knocked him sideways.

'Well, hello, there. Is Iain with you?' she asked.

'No, my mum's babysitting,' he explained. 'And my mum's not the kind of person you argue with, once she gets an idea into her head.' He rolled his eyes. 'She thinks a night out will do me good.'

'Maybe she's right,' Beatrice said. 'It's obvious to me how much you love your son, but parenting is hard—and being a single parent is even harder. Sometimes you need to make time to do something for you.'

'Maybe,' he said.

'Welcome to the team. I really hope you're good at this,' she said, 'because you need to make up for me.'

He'd wondered if she was really as hopeless as she claimed; but then her first ball went straight down the gutter. So did the second.

'Sorry, guys. I'm a bit better at emergency medicine than I am at this,' she said with a rueful smile.

He wanted to give her a hug, but settled for putting up the bumper bars for her. She zig-zagged her way to a half-strike, everyone on their team cheered, and it encouraged her enough that she managed a full strike on her next turn.

'Has anyone actually taught you how to bowl before?' he asked.

'Um, no,' she admitted. 'It's not the kind of thing I normally do.'

'Would you let me help you?'

She looked worried. 'Are you sure that's OK? The other team aren't going to say you're cheating?'

He grinned. ''Course it's OK. Let's start with the ball. You might be better off using a lighter one than the one you picked—which isn't me patronising you,' he said quickly.

'No, it's you explaining properly,' she said. 'Which is an important skill at work, and I wouldn't expect anything less from you.'

He inclined his head in acknowledgement of the compliment; but it warmed him all the way through that she thought that highly of him. 'You stand behind the line, bring your arm back behind you, then bring it forward and let the ball go—try and aim for the middle of the pins. The ball will follow the line of where you let it go,' he said, 'which is why you're zig-zagging. You're leaving it just that little bit too late to let it go.'

She tried a couple of practice bowls, which went horribly wrong. 'Maybe I'd better stick to medicine,' she said.

'No, you can do this. Do you mind if I help guide your arm?' he asked, knowing even as he said it that he really shouldn't let himself get that physically close to her.

'OK.'

Keep this professional. You're helping her bowl a ball, not holding her as if she's your date, he reminded himself silently. He stood behind her, and helped her bring her arm back to the right position, then helped her move forward. 'And now let go.'

'That's amazing! It didn't zig-zag,' she said, her tone full of wonder and delight as the ball went straight down the middle of the lane. 'Thank you.'

And then she turned round and hugged him.

He hugged her back before he realised what he was doing.

Oh, help. This was bad. Really bad. Because Beatrice Lindford fitted perfectly in his arms. And he liked the feel of her arms round him, too.

But he wasn't in a position to start anything with her. Even if she wasn't sort of his boss, there was Iain to consider. How could he get involved with her? If things went wrong between them, and Iain had got close to her, it would devastate the little boy. And, even though she'd been good with his son at the football day, there was a huge difference between helping out at a team event and having a small child as part of your life. Who was to say she even wanted children?

As if she sensed the sudden tension in him, she blushed and let him go. 'Sorry. I got a bit carried away with actually bowling properly for the first time ever.'

'No problem,' he fibbed.

He managed to keep a little bit of physical distance between them for the rest of the evening, even when they stopped midway through the game for tortilla chips, chicken wings and hot dogs. But then his fingers accidentally brushed against hers when they each dipped a tortilla chip into the guacamole, and his heart actually skipped a beat.

He couldn't help looking at her. Her eyes had widened, her pupils were huge and her lips were slightly parted. So did she feel it, too, this weird pull of attraction?

Well, they weren't going to act on it.

He concentrated on the bowling, and the evening went incredibly quickly.

But, at the end of the evening, his mouth decided it had had enough of playing by his brain's rules, and he found himself asking, 'Can I walk you home?'

She looked at him. 'Am I on your way?'

This was his get-out. 'Where are you?'

She told him her address.

'No,' he admitted. But then his mouth took over from his common sense again. 'Though I'd like to walk you home.'

Her smile was slow, sweet, and felt as if it had poleaxed him. 'I'd like that. Thank you.'

On the way back to her place, his hand brushed against hers. He wasn't quite sure how it happened but, the next thing he knew, his fingers were twining round hers and they were holding hands properly.

She didn't say a word, but it wasn't an awkward silence.

How long had it been since he'd last held hands with someone? He thought back. It must've been with Jenny, before Iain was born. When they were still expectant parents, still in love, still thinking that the future was rosy and bright. Before her postnatal depression ripped their new little family apart.

She stopped outside a gate. 'This is my flat,' she said.

It was in one of the beautiful Edwardian townhouses that overlooked the park.

'Very nice,' he said.

'You could come in for a coffee, if you like,' she said.

It was tempting. So very tempting.

But it wouldn't be fair to her to start something that he knew he couldn't finish.

'Thanks, but...'

'But no thanks,' she finished. 'I understand.'

But there had been a flash of hurt in her eyes. It made him want to make her feel better. And all his common sense went out of the window, because he wrapped his arms round her. Lowered his mouth to hers. Brushed his lips against hers once, twice...

Her hands were in his hair and she was kissing him back when he came to his senses again and broke the kiss.

'I'm sorry. That wasn't fair of me,' he said.

'I'm not in a position to date anyone. I have Iain to think of.'

'I know. And I'm not looking to date anyone. I'm concentrating on my career.'

Why was someone as lovely as Beatrice Lindford single in the first place? Daniel had the feeling that someone had hurt her—as much as Jenny had hurt him—but he didn't have the right to ask.

'If my situation was different,' he said, 'I'd ask you out properly.'

'And I'd turn you down, because I'd still be concentrating on my career.'

Whoever had hurt her had *really* hurt her, he thought.

And she'd just been really kind to him. Taken away the guilt.

'Message understood,' he said. 'Goodnight, Beatrice.'

'Goodnight, Daniel. I'll see you at work. And thank you for walking me home.'

'Pleasure,' he said. 'See you at work.'

And he turned away before he did something stupid. Like asking her to change both their minds.

CHAPTER FOUR

SOMEHOW DANIEL WAS going to have to scrub that kiss out of his head.

He couldn't get involved with Beatrice. The sensible side of him knew that. She was his senior at work, so it could be awkward. Their backgrounds were poles apart—she was from a posh family, and he couldn't see them being happy to accept him as Beatrice's partner, not when he was a single dad, and also the illegitimate son of a teenage mum who'd gone massively off the rails. He'd been brought up by his grandparents until he was ten and his mother had settled down again. He didn't have a problem with his past; he was proud of the way Susan had turned her life around. But he also knew that not everyone would share his views.

And most importantly there was Iain.

What if he let Beatrice get close to Iain

and things didn't work out? It would devastate his son. It was hard enough for Iain, dividing himself between his parents. The little boy didn't need any extra calls on his heart from someone who might not stick around.

So it was obvious that Daniel needed to keep things strictly business between himself and Beatrice. For all their sakes.

Dropping Iain over at Jenny's for their usual alternate weekend together occupied part of Saturday morning, but the rest of the day dragged. Cleaning the bathroom, catching up with the laundry, doing the grocery shopping: none of it kept his mind off Beatrice or how it had felt to kiss her. How his lips had tingled. How he'd wanted to draw her closer. How he'd actually forgotten that they were in the street, in full view of any passers-by, because his head had been full of starbursts.

Saturday evening was worse. Why on earth hadn't he made sure he was working both days while Iain was at his mother's for the weekend? Several times Daniel picked up his phone—which was totally pointless as he didn't actually know Beatrice's number, and besides which she'd told him that she was focusing on her career and wasn't interested in a relationship with anyone.

What was wrong with him?

For four years now he'd focused on his son. He'd turned down offers of dates. Women hadn't appeared on his radar other than as friends, colleagues or patients. He hadn't wanted to get involved with anyone.

Why had Beatrice Lindford got him in such a spin? What was so different about her? Why couldn't he get her out of his head? The questions went round and round his head, and he just couldn't find an answer.

Somehow Beatrice was going to have to scrub that kiss out of her head.

She couldn't get involved with Daniel. Iain was almost the same age that Taylor would've been; he was a gorgeous little boy, but every time she saw him she'd remember her lost little girl, and the pain would rip another layer off her scar tissue. She wasn't sure she was ready for a relationship with anyone, let alone with someone who had a small child. Plus, if she told Daniel about her past, would he assume that she only wanted to get involved with him so she'd have a ready-made family to help fill the hole in her life?

This couldn't work. Not in a month of Sundays.

And what was it about Daniel that drew her so much? Yes, he was physically attractive, but she'd met plenty of attractive men since she'd split up with Oliver. She just hadn't really noticed any of them. Hadn't dated any of them. Hadn't wanted to get involved with any of them.

But Daniel Capaldi was different.

She'd felt that weird awareness right from the start, even when he'd been slightly frosty towards her. As he'd started to thaw out towards her, she'd found herself thinking of him more and more often.

Then he'd kissed her on Friday night, and every nerve ending in her body had reacted.

And it had scared the hell out of her. She couldn't remember the last time she'd reacted like that to anyone—even to Oliver, because her emotions had just shut down after Taylor's death.

She was pretty sure it was the same for Daniel, because he'd looked dazed when he'd broken the kiss. And he'd used his son as an excuse why they couldn't see each other.

She'd come straight out with the excuse that she wasn't dating, she was concentrating on her career.

The whole thing was like a house of cards. Fragile. So easy to fall apart.

She didn't want to risk getting involved again. Getting hurt again. Losing her heart again.

So she needed to keep things strictly business between herself and Daniel.

It wasn't working.

Even though Sunday had been busy at work—and thankfully Beatrice had been off duty—and the evening had been taken up with Iain chattering about what he'd done at the weekend with his mum and Jordan, Daniel just couldn't get that kiss out of his head.

Worse still, every time he caught Beatrice's eye at work on Monday, there was a fleeting expression on her face that made him pretty sure she was remembering that kiss. That she, too, was in this weird state where her head was telling her this was a bad idea but she still wanted to repeat it anyway.

What was he going to do?

After another night spent fitfully waking

from dreams of Beatrice—dreams where they were dancing together, holding each other, kissing—Daniel came to a decision in the shower.

He needed help.

Ironically, he thought the best person to help him would be the same person who'd caused him a problem in the first place: Beatrice herself. Maybe if he told her about his past, explained about what had happened with Jenny when Iain was tiny, then she'd help him to be sensible and keep things platonic between them.

They were both rostered on Minors that day, so he was pretty sure they'd be able to take their lunch break together.

'Can we have a chat over lunch?' he asked when he saw her in the staff kitchen during their break.

She looked slightly wary. 'A chat?'

'Somewhere quiet. Maybe a sandwich in the park, as it's a nice day?' he suggested.

She still looked wary. 'A chat.'

'To clear the air,' he said.

'All right,' she said eventually.

'Meet you at twelve-thirty, here?' he asked.

'OK. Twelve-thirty,' she said, 'depending on our patients' needs.'

'Of course,' he said.

He made it through the morning; and then he headed for the staff kitchen to meet Beatrice. She was already there. 'Still OK for a sandwich and some fresh air?' he asked.

'Sure,' she said.

They bought sandwiches from the hospital canteen, then went out to the park in a slightly uneasy silence.

'I owe you an explanation,' he said when they found a quiet bench and sat down.

She shook her head. 'You don't owe me anything.'

'I think I do. And the best way I can do that is to explain about my situation,' he said. 'About Iain.'

Did that mean he wanted her to explain her situation, too? Beatrice wondered. Because she wasn't prepared for that. She didn't want to talk about losing her baby, or the way her marriage had collapsed, and she definitely didn't want to talk about what she'd done. But she'd listen to what he had to say.

'Obviously I'll keep anything you say in confidence,' she said.

'I've worked at Muswell Hill Memorial Hospital for long enough that pretty much everyone knows what happened,' Daniel said dryly. 'But thank you.'

Not quite knowing what to say next, she waited.

'Jenny—my ex-wife—had serious postnatal depression after Iain was born,' he said. 'I let her down. I should've picked up on it a lot sooner than I did.'

'You're not being fair to yourself. You work in emergency medicine, not obstetrics or general practice,' she reminded him.

He shrugged. 'Even so, I should've noticed that it was more than just the baby blues that you hear people talking about. That she wasn't sleeping well and she was really tired, and it wasn't just because she was getting up at night to feed the baby. That she was feeling low, and it was more than just the usual worries a new parent has about whether you're going to be good enough. That she worried and worried about whether Iain was all right. That she checked him in his cot a bit too often, to make sure he was still breathing.'

Would she have been like that if Taylor had lived? Beatrice wondered. Worrying constantly, checking on the baby?

She forced the thoughts away and tried to concentrate on what Daniel was telling her.

He blew out a breath. 'I was busy at work, so I didn't pay Jenny enough attention. I didn't notice that she was gradually withdrawing from everyone. I didn't ask her enough about her day or notice that she made excuses not to meet up with the other mums from our antenatal group. I didn't see that she wasn't coping.'

'You can't put all the blame on yourself,' she said. 'As you said, you were working, so you weren't with her all the time. Even if you weren't getting up to do any of the night feeds, when Iain woke and screamed it probably woke you, so you weren't getting enough sleep either. You were tired and trying to do your best. Plus you weren't the only one to see Jenny. What about her family, her friends, her health visitor? Didn't they say anything?'

'Her best friend did,' Daniel said. 'She noticed Jenny didn't wash her hair as much as she used to, and she didn't dress the way she used to before Iain arrived. I'd noticed, too, but I assumed it was just because she was adjusting to a new routine with the baby and I wasn't going to pressure her to look super-glamorous every second of the day.'

Beatrice liked the fact Daniel was so sensitive. After Taylor's funeral, Oliver had expected her to dress up and keep going to his office functions. She'd forced herself to do it, not wanting to let him down any further than she already had. Inside, she'd been falling apart; outside, she'd kept the stiff upper lip expected from her by everyone. In the end, it hadn't made a difference. Going along with the same routine, smiling at people and pretending that everything was all right simply hadn't made everything all right. It had just made her bottle everything up until she finally broke down.

'She'd lost her sense of humour,' Daniel continued, 'and I just put it down to the stresses of being a new mum. I didn't pay enough attention.'

'It's harder to spot when you see someone every day and when it's a gradual change,' Beatrice pointed out.

'I still should have noticed,' Daniel insisted. And she could see the guilt racking him, reflected in his dark eyes. 'And then one day, when Iain was about two months old, I got home from work and she wasn't there. Iain was lying in his cot, screaming his head off. I changed his nappy and fed him—thankfully we'd got a bottle and some cartons of baby milk in case of emergency—and I called her, but her phone was switched off. I tried her mum, her sister, her friends from work, just about everyone in our phone book, but nobody had heard from her or seen her that day.'

Beatrice sucked in a breath. She'd done the same thing, two months after the accident. Waited until she had a day when she thought she wouldn't be disturbed. Except her intentions had been a lot more final. If Victoria, her sister-in-law, hadn't knocked on her door and refused to take silence for an answer...

She pulled herself together, this wasn't about her. It was about Daniel and Iain and Jenny. 'That must've been really hard for you,' she said.

He nodded. 'If she'd taken Iain with her, I wouldn't have been quite so worried. I would've thought maybe she was having coffee with a friend and had forgotten the time. But the fact that she'd left Iain on his own—I didn't think she'd just popped out to get a pint of milk or something while he was asleep. She would've taken him with her. I thought she might have…' He tailed off, his expression full of pain.

He didn't have to finish the sentence. Beatrice knew exactly what he meant. He'd thought that Jenny might have done exactly what Beatrice herself had done.

'I reported her to the police as missing, and I put stuff all over social media in case someone saw her, begging them to let me know—I just needed to know she was safe. Obviously I called work and said I needed emergency parental leave until Jenny was home. And my mum flew down from Glasgow the next morning to help out with Iain while I pestered everyone I knew and tried to find Jenny.'

His family had rallied round, Beatrice thought. Hers—even her sisters-in-law— had panicked and refused to talk about what she'd done. Pretending it hadn't happened meant they didn't have to face the fear that she might do it again.

'What happened?' she asked.

'I was tearing my hair out. But three days later someone at a hotel recognised her from a photograph I'd put on social media and called the police, who brought her home. I was just so relieved she hadn't…'

'Yes,' Beatrice said softly. She'd put her family through just as much worry as Jenny had, and it still made her feel guilty.

'Anyway, I got her an appointment with our family doctor and Mum looked after Iain while I went with her to support her.' He grimaced. 'I asked her why she'd left him—I wasn't going to judge her, because I knew it was so out of character. I just wanted to understand, so I could help her. And I was so shocked when she said she'd thought she was going to do something to hurt him because he wouldn't stop crying and she didn't know what to do—she left to keep him safe.'

'I can understand that,' Beatrice said. 'If you're already low with postnatal depression and you're panicking that everything's going wrong, a crying baby would send you over the edge.' In her case, though, it had been the opposite. She would've given anything to hear her baby cry. It was the lack of crying, the lack of anything, the sheer *emptiness* that had tipped her over the edge. 'And I'm guessing she knew you'd be back relatively soon and would be there for him.'

He nodded. 'She thought he'd probably

cry himself to sleep. Maybe he did; and maybe he woke up again just before I got back. I don't know.'

'And the doctor helped?'

'He gave her antidepressants as well as referring her for CBT. Jenny's parents live miles away in the Cotswolds, so Mum moved down from Glasgow permanently to help support us.' He blew out a breath. 'She got better over the next few months, but things between us were terrible. I felt guilty for not supporting her better; I felt angry with her for leaving him alone when he couldn't look after himself and something could've happened to him; and I felt guilty for being angry because I knew it wasn't her fault that she was ill and her judgement wasn't what it normally was. But no matter how much I tried I couldn't get past it; it was like a vicious circle that spiralled tighter and tighter. We couldn't seem to find our way back to how things were before Iain was born. It was as if all the love we'd shared just drained away and there was nothing left.'

Beatrice knew exactly how that felt.

'In the end we split up and she agreed I could have custody of Iain.'

'Does she see him at all?'

'Yes, he stays with her every other weekend. He stayed with her this weekend. But that's why I don't want to get involved with anyone—Iain's already had a rough start, and it's up to me to give him stability.'

'Is Jenny involved with anyone?'

He nodded. 'She remarried a year ago. We talked about the custody situation with Iain and, even though he's older now and it's fine between them, she doesn't trust herself not to let him down again. I'm never going to withhold access or anything spiteful like that, because she's his mum and I want him to know her and love her as much as she loves him—but I'm the one who looks after him, with support from my mum, and that's the way it's going to stay.'

Beatrice had been in that same dark place—except she'd never see Taylor grow up, the way Jenny would see Iain change from a child to a young man. She and Oliver had been in the same vicious circle as Daniel and Jenny except, unlike Daniel, Oliver hadn't tried to understand why his wife had tried to get out of the situation. And, instead of talking about it, or getting her to talk, he'd taken the stiff upper lip approach;

in his view, if they didn't discuss it, it hadn't happened.

The cracks had grown wider and wider; and finally Beatrice had had the strength to leave him and let him find happiness with someone else.

Maybe she should tell Daniel. Given his own experiences, she was pretty sure he would understand. But she also thought he'd see her differently, once he knew what she'd done. She didn't want him to pity her or avoid her—not now, when they were starting to gel as a team at work.

'I'm sorry you've all been through so much,' she said.

'We're good now,' Daniel said, 'but I don't want to risk ever being in that position again.'

Which made her the last person he'd ever want to get involved with. Her own depression wasn't quite the same as Jenny's, but it had similar roots. She'd been on Jenny's side of the illness. And what if they did get together and her depression returned? She'd be letting him down—and she'd be letting his son down, too. Daniel hadn't been able to forgive Jenny, so it was pretty clear that he wouldn't be able to forgive Beatrice, either.

It was better to stick to being colleagues. 'Thank you for telling me. As I said, I won't be gossiping about you.'

'I appreciate that.'

A little voice inside her head said, *Tell him*.

But she just couldn't.

Instead, she said brightly, 'I guess we'd better be getting back to the department. The waiting room's probably filled while we've been at lunch.'

'Agreed,' Daniel said.

And if she kept reminding herself that this thing between her and Daniel couldn't even start, she'd come to believe it.

CHAPTER FIVE

For the rest of the week, Daniel managed to keep everything between himself and Beatrice completely professional.

But then, on Friday lunchtime, he was just grabbing a coffee from the staff kitchen when his phone beeped.

The message was from his childminder.

Daniel, please ring me urgently.

He frowned. Diane rarely texted him. Something was obviously wrong.

His heart skipped a beat. *Iain.*

No, it couldn't be. Iain was at school. They would've called Daniel straight away, not Diane—wouldn't they?

He called her immediately. 'Diane, it's Daniel. What's happened?'

'It's my mum,' Diane said.

And how horrible was he that relief flooded through him? Not Iain. His precious son was all right.

'She collapsed and she's being taken to hospital.'

'Here? I'll keep an eye out for her and ask to make sure she sees me.'

'No, she lives in Essex.' Her voice shook. 'They don't know what's wrong. It might be a stroke. I need to be with her, so I won't be able to pick Iain up from school today.'

Which left him with a huge problem. But Diane had enough to worry about, with her mum's health, so he wasn't going to make things worse for her. 'Of course you need to be with your mum. Don't worry. I'll sort something out for Iain. Let me know if there's anything I can do to help or if you want the medics there to talk to me.'

'Oh, Daniel.' She sounded close to tears. 'Thank you for being so nice about it.'

'No problem,' he fibbed. There wasn't exactly anything else he could be other than nice. 'Take care, and I hope your mum is okay. Let me know how she's getting on.'

He frowned as he ended the call. What was he going to do now? Normally he would have called on his mother, but Susan was away in Birmingham, running a three-day course, and she wouldn't be back until tomorrow. Jenny was leaving work early because she was going away for the weekend, so he couldn't ask her to help, either. And if he asked for unpaid leave it would mean the department was short-staffed, which wasn't fair on the team.

There had to be someone he could ask. Someone who knew Iain. Maybe he could ask the mum of one of Iain's friends to take him home for a few hours, until he'd finished his shift?

At that moment, the kitchen door opened and Beatrice walked in.

'Are you all right?' she asked.

'Yes—well, no,' he admitted. There wasn't any point in lying. 'My childminder's mother just collapsed so she can't pick Iain up from school. Mum's running a course in Birmingham and Jenny's away.' He raked a hand through his hair. 'I'm just going to have to call round the mums of Iain's friends and see if any of them can help me out.'

Beatrice knew that this was her cue to wish Daniel luck, make herself a coffee and let him get on with it. But he looked worried sick. How could she just turn her back on him, when he clearly needed help?

There was an obvious solution. Part of her thought it was a bad idea, tantamount to getting involved with him. And having a four-year-old child in her flat—a child the age her daughter would've been—was that really a good idea? Wouldn't it just rip the top of her scars?

Then again, what was the difference between George, her four-year-old nephew, and Iain? Plus she'd met Iain and they'd got on just fine.

It would be the best solution for both Iain and Daniel. And, as Daniel's senior, she needed to support him. Right?

Before she could talk herself out of it, she said, 'I'm off duty at three. I could pick him up for you.'

He blinked. 'You? But…'

'I'd do the same for any colleague who was a bit stuck and needed help,' she said. 'Iain knows me. I don't think he'll mind me looking after him for the afternoon. And I can take him back to my place—I've got a box of toys and books for my niece and nephews, so I'm sure we can find something he'll enjoy in there.'

'That's very kind of you, but I'm on a late. I can't swap shifts.'

'It's not a problem. Iain can have dinner with me,' she said. 'Any allergies I need to know about?'

Daniel raked a hand through his hair again, and the dishevelment made him look absolutely scrumptious. *Colleagues,* she reminded herself sharply. They were colleagues. With her past, she was the very last woman that he needed to get involved with.

'No allergies,' he said. 'Are you quite sure it's not going to cause you any hassle? You might already have plans for tonight.'

'I don't have any plans,' she said. Not because she wanted him to know that her social life was pared down—or why—but because she didn't want him feeling guilty. 'It's fine. I guess you'll need to contact his school to let them know I'm picking Iain up with your permission. If you want to send them a photo of my work ID card, that's fine. And I'll need the school's address and your mobile number, and you'll obviously need my details.'

'Thank you,' he said. 'I owe you.'

She shook her head. 'From what I've seen so far of the department here, it's like my old one at the Hampstead Free. Everyone mucks in and helps each other. It all evens out in the end.'

'It'd be a huge weight off my mind,' he admitted.

'Well, then. Let's get it sorted out.'

It didn't take long for Daniel to arrange things with the school and send them a copy of Beatrice's work ID, and to synchronise information with Beatrice.

And so, at the end of her shift, Beatrice found herself heading for the local infant school.

School.

Taylor, like Iain, would have been in her first year at school. A summer-born child, about to turn five: one of the younger members of the class. If life had gone to plan, Beatrice would have been working part time so she could take her daughter to school and pick her up.

But it hadn't worked out that way.

And she couldn't afford to let herself think about what she'd lost. What she'd never have now.

Besides, it wouldn't be the first time she'd picked up a child from school. She'd met all her nephews and her niece from school, on more than one occasion. She could do this.

She hung back in the playground as the children filed out of the class to join their parents or carers, feeling out of place, but finally Iain appeared at the doorway, holding his teacher's hand.

'Bee!' he called, waving his free hand. 'Miss Fisher said you'd be here!'

She was pleased to note that Miss Fisher kept him by her side, rather than letting the little boy run over to her. She went over and showed her ID. 'I'm Beatrice Lindford and I work with Daniel,' she said.

'He told us to expect you, Dr Lindford.' Miss Fisher looked at Iain. 'Are you happy to go home with Dr Lindford?' she checked.

The little boy nodded. 'She's the one I told you about, the one who fixed my arm when I falled over at football. She's nice. I drawed that picture of her.'

'Which has pride of place on the outside of my fridge right now,' Beatrice said. 'Let's go, and you can tell me what your favourite food is so I can make it for tea.'

'Pasta!' Daniel said happily.

'Pasta it shall be,' she said.

It didn't take long to walk back to her

place. Iain was thrilled to see his drawing on her fridge. 'Who drawed the other pictures? Do you have a little boy or girl?'

A little girl. *Born asleep.*

She pushed the wave of misery back. This wasn't something to dump on a small child. 'That one was drawn by my niece, Seffy,' she said, pointing to a picture of a horse.

'Seffy? That's a funny name,' Iain commented.

'It's short for Persephone.'

'Pu-sef…' He stumbled over the name.

'Persephone,' Beatrice said. 'And that's her pony.'

His eyes went wide. 'She has a pony?'

'Because she lives in the country,' Beatrice hastened to add. The last thing she wanted was to cause Daniel problems, if Iain turned out to be as pony-mad as Seffy was. 'And this train was drawn by my nephew George. He's four, just like you.'

'It's a good train,' Iain said politely. 'I like trains.'

'So do I,' Beatrice said. 'And I have a train set. And dinosaurs,' she added, remembering what Daniel had told her. 'Let's get you a glass of milk and some fruit to keep you going until teatime, and then we can play with the trains and the dinosaurs, if you like.'

'Yes!' Iain said. And then he looked horrified. 'Please,' he added.

'Excellent,' Beatrice said with a smile, and busied herself slicing up an apple. While Iain was drinking his milk, she prepared a tomato sauce and left it to simmer on the hob.

She thoroughly enjoyed making a train track with him through a world of dinosaurs, and took a picture of him on her phone to send to Daniel as reassurance that the little boy was settled and not fretting.

Iain loved the pasta and sauce, to her relief. And then she looked at him. 'I haven't got anything for pudding. Shall we make some cake?'

'Chocolate cake?' he asked hopefully. 'Like the ones you made for football?'

'The brownies? We can do that,' she said with a smile. 'You can be chief mixer.'

'Yay!' he said, looking thrilled.

She set him up with a tea towel as a makeshift apron to keep his clothes clean, then helped him weigh out the dry ingredients into a bowl and the wet ingredients into a jug. 'And now you just mix them together with a spoon until it's all gloopy.'

She loved baking with her niece and nephews at Beresford, and she enjoyed her cooking session with Iain just as much.

Fortified with a warm brownie and another glass of milk, Iain cuddled up to her on the sofa and fell asleep while she read him one of George's favourite stories.

She put the book down but didn't move, not wanting to wake him; luckily it was a warm evening so she didn't need to get a blanket for him. Was this what it would have been like with Taylor—curled up together on the sofa on a Friday night, waiting for Oliver to come home from work?

But it was pointless, wishing. Oliver's love for her hadn't survived the loss of the baby, just as her love for him had leaked away. They both had a new life now. Oliver was happy with his new wife—and with their new baby son. And Beatrice was doing just fine.

When her phone pinged, the message was from Daniel.

On way to pick him up. Be with you in ten minutes.

She woke Iain gently. 'Your dad's on his way to pick you up.'

He cuddled into her. 'I had a nice time today. Thank you for looking after me.'

'My pleasure,' she said, and she meant it. Even though having a child around had brought back her old regrets about what might have been, she'd enjoyed his company.

Daniel rang her doorbell ten minutes later.

'He's fine, he's been a total sweetheart, and you really don't have to worry,' she said.

'You got me out of a real hole. Thank you—I really appreciate it,' he said, and handed her a bunch of flowers. 'Sorry they're only supermarket ones, but it was all I could get at this time of night.'

He'd actually taken time out to get these for her? Her heart melted. 'They're lovely, though you really didn't need to,' she said. 'Have you eaten?'

'I'm fine,' he said.

Meaning he hadn't. Was he fudging the issue because he didn't want to impose on her any further, or did he not want to spend any more time here than he had to?

'I've got spare pasta and sauce from earlier,' she said. 'It'll take a couple of minutes in the microwave. Take it with you if you'd rather not eat right now.'

Oh, help.

When she looked at him with those big blue eyes... It would be so easy to say yes. To lose his head.

'We had pasta for tea and it was yummy,' Iain said, running over to him and hugging him.

Take it home, she mouthed out of Iain's eyeline.

Thank you, he mouthed back, and wrapped his arms round his son. 'I need to get you home to bed, young man.'

'We made brownies, Dad. The best chocolate brownies in the world.'

The kind of cake Daniel really didn't like. He hated the cloying sweetness. And if there was oily buttercream in the middle...

'We saved you some,' Iain said.

There was absolutely no way he could get out of this. Not without disappointing his son and making Iain feel pushed away and he'd never do that. So he'd just have to smile and choke it down.

'I'll cut you a small piece,' Beatrice said, as if she guessed what he was thinking. Or, more likely, it was written all over his face but Iain was that bit too young to decipher his expression.

'Thank you,' he said.

But, to Daniel's surprise, the cake wasn't sticky and oversweet and vile. It was light and dense at the same time, chocolatey without being too sugary. 'This is fantastic,' he said.

'Take some more home. I'm not going to be able to eat the rest over the weekend.'

'My granny's coming home tomorrow. Can I take some for her?' Iain asked, adding a belated, 'Please?'

'Sure you can,' she said, and wrapped up several pieces in greaseproof paper. She put the pasta and sauce into a plastic lidded box. 'Put it in the microwave for three minutes on full power, stir, and then give it another minute,' she said to Daniel.

'I… I don't know what to say,' he said.

'I'd do the same for any of my colleagues,' she said, 'as I'm sure you would, too.'

True. Except he still couldn't get himself to think of Beatrice as strictly his colleague. He still remembered what it had felt like to kiss her. How sweet her mouth had been.

How good it had felt to walk along the street holding hands with her.

He needed to leave. Now. Before he did or said something stupid.

'Thank you for having me,' Iain said, and hugged her.

'My pleasure. I enjoyed having you here to play trains with me,' Beatrice said.

'Next time, can George come, too?' Iain asked.

George? She had a son?

Daniel shook himself mentally. Of course she didn't. She'd told him about her nephew. The one who had a less unusual name.

Before he could correct Iain and explain that it was rude to invite yourself to someone's house, Beatrice said, 'I'll see what I can do.'

Iain hugged her again.

'Let's get your things,' she said, and helped him on with his shoes.

Seeing her with him like that made Daniel ache; it made him realise how much Jenny's postnatal depression had taken away from all of them. And it brought out his own doubts: was he enough for Iain? Should he be trying to find someone who would be a mum to Iain when he wasn't at Jenny's? Daniel had vowed he wouldn't get involved with anyone again, but was he being selfish? Surely he should put his son's needs first?

'I'll see you at work on Monday,' Beatrice said with a smile, as if completely oblivious to what was whirling round in his head. Or maybe she was too kind to broach the subject.

'Yes. Thanks again for having Iain.'

'Any time.'

Was she just being polite or did she mean it? He had no idea.

Iain, now he was awake, chattered about how wonderful Beatrice was—all the way home, all the way through two bedtime stories, and he would have kept going all night if Daniel hadn't said to him, 'It's time to sleep or you'll be too tired to go to the park tomorrow.'

'Football?' Iain asked hopefully.

'Football,' Daniel promised.

When he finally sat down, Daniel was almost too tired to eat. He was grateful for the fact that Beatrice had saved him some pasta. And the sauce was definitely home-made rather than just heated through from a jar.

Beatrice Lindford was a puzzle.

She'd been adamant that she wasn't looking for a relationship and she was concentrating on her career. And yet the way she'd been with Iain—picking him up from school without a fuss, cooking him his favourite dinner, playing with him and reading with him—those were the actions of a woman who was used to being part of a family. OK, so she'd hinted that she was close to her brothers and their children; but what had happened to Beatrice to make her so determined not to date and have a family of her own?

Asking her felt too intrusive, especially when she'd just done him such a huge favour. It was none of his business. Besides, they were supposed to be keeping their distance from each other, not getting closer. He needed to back off.

The next morning, Iain was still talking about Beatrice.

He didn't change the topic of conversation when his grandmother came home, either. 'Granny, Granny, me and Bee maked you some cake!'

'Bee?' Susan looked mystified.

'You know, Princess Bee, who fixed my arm when I falled over.'

'Why were you making cake with her?'

'Diane couldn't pick me up from school and Dad was working, so Bee gave me my tea and played trains with me. And we maked cake.'

Susan gave Daniel a look that meant they were going to have a talk, later. One that was going to make him squirm.

'They're chocolate brownies. Dad liked them. I brought some home for you.'

'Let's give Granny her cake,' Daniel said, hoping that it might distract his mother but knowing that it probably wouldn't.

'You're right, this is excellent chocolate cake,' Susan said after her first taste. 'I hope you remembered to say thank you to Bea, Daniel.'

'I did. And Dad gave her flowers.'

Daniel had hoped that Iain had been too tired or too excited to notice. But not only did Iain have eyes like a hawk, he was intent on telling every detail to everyone who would listen.

'Flowers? That's nice.' Susan gave him an arch look. 'But, Iain, if someone invites us for dinner, we have to be polite and invite them back for dinner.'

Oh, no. Daniel could see exactly where this was going. 'Mum, she works in my department and she's my senior. She won't have time.'

'You don't know unless you ask her.'

Which wasn't the worst thing she could have said, in Daniel's view. He knew that Iain wouldn't budge from the subject until he gave in; which meant Bea would be put on the spot. Unless Daniel texted her to warn her, and suggested that she tell Iain she was working...

Before he had the chance—and no doubt his mother had already guessed what he was thinking and was pre-empting him— Susan said, 'I think you should ask her to tea, Iain. Tomorrow. Her number's in your dad's phone, isn't it?'

Iain squeaked with excitement and grabbed Daniel's phone.

'She might be w—' Daniel began.

But Iain was too excited by the idea to listen and thrust the phone at him. 'Call her now, Dad, and I'll ask her.'

What could Daniel do, other than hope that her phone went through to voicemail?

He unlocked his phone, set up the call, and handed the phone to Iain.

'Hello, Bea. Will you come to tea tomorrow?'

Say no, Daniel thought. Say no.

'Yes, it's Iain. How did you know? Your phone told you it was my dad? Oh. Will you come to tea?'

Iain paused, clearly waiting for an answer, then frowned. 'I don't know. What time, Granny?'

'Six,' Susan said.

'Six,' Iain repeated.

'Ask her if she likes Scottish roast beef,' Susan prompted.

'Granny says, do you like Scottish roast beef?' Iain asked. Then he smiled. 'She does, Granny. And she says she'll bring some apple crumble to go with it.'

'Tell her thank you,' Susan said.

'Thank you,' Iain said. 'See you tomorrow.'

'I think you need to go and tidy your toys,' Susan said when Iain handed the phone back to Daniel.

'I will, Granny,' Iain said, and rushed off.

'Don't go getting any ideas, Mum,' Daniel warned. 'Beatrice is my colleague, as good as my boss. I was in a jam and she helped me out—just as she would have helped out anyone else in the department.'

'Hmm,' Susan said.

'We're *colleagues*,' Daniel insisted.

Beatrice texted him half an hour later.

Just checking. Is tomorrow OK or would you rather I make an excuse?

He could have kissed her. The perfect let-out. She could make an excuse…

But then Iain would be so disappointed. And also, if his mother met Beatrice and saw for herself that they really were just colleagues, then maybe she could help persuade Iain to back off a little bit.

It's fine. See you tomorrow, he texted back. Better give you the address.

Iain was almost beyond excited, the next day, when Beatrice arrived, and greeted her with a squeal and a hug.

'It's lovely to meet you, Bea. I'm Susan, Daniel's mother,' Susan said.

'Thank you for asking me over. It's kind of you to cook for me, especially as I'm sure you must be tired after your course,' Beatrice said.

'Daniel told you about me?'

'Not much. Just that you were an artist. Y chromosomes,' Beatrice added in a stage whisper, and Susan laughed and patted her arm.

Uh-oh. That looked as if two people from his immediate family had bonded with her almost instantly, Daniel thought.

'Come and sit down,' Susan said, ushering her to the kitchen.

Daniel gave in to the inevitable and followed them. 'I'll make some coffee,' he said.

'I hope you like apple crumble, Iain,' Beatrice said. 'I made this with our own apples.' She put the dish on the table.

'Our?' Susan asked. 'You have an orchard?'

'My parents do. I went to see my family yesterday,' she explained, 'and I raided the stores.'

'Bee's family lives in the country and her niece has got a pony,' Iain informed them.

Daniel could see the intrigued expression in his mother's eyes and headed her off by talking about her course.

'So what sort of thing do you paint, Susan?' Beatrice asked.

'Granny's done loads of paintings. Come and see,' Iain said, and tugged at Beatrice's hand. 'Granny lets me paint with her, sometimes.'

'Don't grill her,' Daniel begged his mother softly when Beatrice left the kitchen.

'As if I would,' Susan said, with an arch look.

Yeah. He was in trouble.

Beatrice duly admired the paintings, and then it was time for dinner.

'This is fabulous. Thank you so much for inviting me,' Beatrice said.

'You can come every Sunday,' Iain said. 'Oh, but not next week because I'm at my mum's.'

'That's kind of you, but it would be greedy of me to eat here every Sunday,' Beatrice said.

'We can take turns. So we can come to you, next time,' Iain answered, his eyes sparkling.

How had this happened? Daniel wondered. Iain hardly knew Beatrice. Shouldn't he be shy and hardly saying a word, instead of chattering away as if he'd known her for ever? This was just what he wanted to avoid: his son getting close to someone who probably wasn't going to stick around.

As if it was written all over his face, and Beatrice had noticed, she said gently, 'That would be nice, because we're friends, your dad and me. Just like he's friends with Josh and Sam and Hayley at the hospital, because we all work together.'

'Oh,' Iain said, but he seemed to accept it.

But, as Beatrice talked to Susan about art and Iain about school, she sparkled, and Daniel found himself spellbound by her.

'The crumble's excellent,' Susan said. 'So were your brownies—thank you for sending me one via Iain. So your parents have a café as well as an orchard?'

'Sort of,' Beatrice said.

He already knew that her family was posh. He had a feeling there was more to it than a café, and he could she was sidestepping the issue.

'My parents had a café in Glasgow,' Susan said. 'An ice cream café. My great-grandparents came to Glasgow from Italy, between the wars, and started the business. My grandparents and then my parents took over.'

'So you have a brother or sister who runs it now?'

'Cousin,' Susan said. 'I'm an only one—like Daniel. But I always wanted to do art. And there's Daniel with medicine. And who knows what Iain will do?'

'I'm going to be a footballer, Granny,' Iain said, rolling his eyes. 'And I'll play for Scotland *and* England. And then I'm going to be an astronaut and go to the moon in a rocket.'

She ruffled his hair. 'You can do anything you put your mind to. I know you have a niece with a pony, Bea, so you're not an only child.'

'I'm the youngest of three,' Beatrice said.

'And your siblings, they're involved in the café?'

Susan steadfastly refused to meet Daniel's gaze, so she completely ignored his mouthed, '*Stop grilling her.*'

'They're involved in the family business,' Beatrice said with a smile. 'We just get the odd scientist in a generation—I'm the one in ours. I take after our great-great-uncle. I was tiny when he died, and I always wish I'd had a chance to get to know him because he's the one who built the telescope in the cupola.'

Iain's eyes went wide. 'You've got a tele-scope?'

'At my parents'.' She nodded. 'I used to spend hours watching the stars. If I hadn't been a doctor, I might've been an astronaut.'

'That's what *I* want to be, after I've been a footballer,' he said. 'Can I show you my rocket Granny painted on my wall?'

'Later,' Daniel said.

'Can I come and see your telescope?' Iain asked.

'I'll see what I can do,' Beatrice told him.

'A telescope in a cupola,' Susan said thoughtfully.

Yes. Daniel had picked that up, too. An architectural feature that, on a family home, marked that family out as more than just or-dinarily posh. He had a nasty feeling that his son's original assessment of Beatrice Lind-ford might be right.

'What's a cupola?' Iain asked.

'It's a dome on a roof,' Beatrice said.

'Like the big one on St Paul's, the place where we whispered to each other from op-posite sides and could hear each other?' Daniel said.

'Do your parents live in a church?' Iain asked.

Beatrice smiled. 'No, sweetheart, they don't.'

'Well, it must be a really big house if it's got a dome,' Iain said. 'Is it a castle? Because you talk like a princess and you've got long golden hair like the princess in the story.'

Beatrice blew out a breath. 'Yes, it's a castle, but I'm not a princess.'

Her family lived in a castle. So the chances were she had a title of some sort. Which put her even more out of his reach, Daniel thought. So much for the orchard and a café: they were clearly part of an estate. A café that perhaps meant her family home was a stately home open to the public?

'Do you know the Queen? And Prince Harry?'

'No.'

Iain looked disappointed. 'My mum likes Prince Harry.'

'Everyone likes Prince Harry,' Beatrice said with a smile. 'Now, once we've had our tea and I've done my share of the washing up, can we play with your train set?'

'Yay!' Iain said.

Daniel was still trying to process it when he helped them build the train track. She was a senior doctor. A woman who had a title. And yet here she was, playing trains on the floor with his son, looking as if she belonged. She'd made friends with his mother almost immediately. She'd wielded a dishcloth in his kitchen.

He and Beatrice were worlds apart. They couldn't possibly have a future.

Or could they?

After Beatrice had left and he'd put Iain to bed, Susan made them both a cup of tea.

'I like her,' she said. 'A lot.'

'Don't get ideas, Mum. We've been through this already. We're colleagues. You heard her say it yourself.'

'You don't look at each other like colleagues.'

'Our backgrounds are too diff—' He stopped and grimaced. 'That came out wrong. I wasn't having a pop at you, Mum.'

'I know. And you have a point. Her family home is a castle. She might not be a princess, but she can probably trace her ancestors all the way back to William the Conqueror—whereas you don't even have your father's name on your birth certificate and you come from working-class stock. But that doesn't matter. I'm proud to be a Capaldi.'

'So am I, Mum.'

'And if that sort of thing does matter to her, then she doesn't deserve you. Though I don't think that sort of thing matters to her.'

'We're not dating, Mum,' he reminded her.

'Maybe you should. Jenny found happiness again. There's no reason why you can't, too.'

Panic flooded through him. But what if it went wrong? 'There's Iain. He's had enough disruption in his life. I'm not prepared to let anyone into his world, only for them to leave him high and dry.'

'Iain adores Bea. And I like her, too. She might be from a posh family, but she's down to earth. She'll get on the floor and play trains with Iain, she'll do baking with him and not mind about the mess, and she's not a haughty mare who won't even pick up a dishcloth—I think you're troubling trouble before it troubles you, and that's never a good thing.' She folded her arms. 'You like her.'

He sighed. 'Yes, I like her.'

'Then do something about it. If you want to protect Iain—not that I think he needs protecting from Bea—then I'll babysit and we don't need to tell Iain where you're going. See how things go.'

Daniel shook his head. 'It's not as easy as that. She doesn't want to get involved either. She's focusing on her career.'

'The way I've seen her with Iain today, she's all about family. I think someone's hurt her—as badly as you got hurt with Jenny.' She put both hands up in a stop gesture. 'I'm not blaming Jenny for anything. I know she was ill. But both of you came out of that marriage with scars. All credit to the pair of you that you never let Iain be aware of them.'

'Yeah.' Daniel sighed. 'I think Beatrice and I will just be colleagues. Maybe friends.'

'Hmm,' Susan said.

'Really, Mum. I can't take that risk. For Iain's sake.'

'I think,' Susan said, 'you're scared and you're hiding behind your son.'

He couldn't argue with her, because he knew she was right. 'I'm not ready,' he said.

She reached over and squeezed his hand. 'I don't think she'll hurt you. There's something about her. An inner strength.'

'Maybe.' But he was pretty sure that Beatrice had been hurt, too. And he hadn't been a good enough support to Jenny. He'd let her down. What was to say he wouldn't let Beatrice down, too, if things went wrong?

CHAPTER SIX

'I'M SORRY ABOUT the grilling,' Daniel said when he saw Beatrice in the staff kitchen the next morning.

'No problem.' She smiled at him. 'I liked your mum.'

'Thanks. She liked you, too.'

The fact that both Daniel's son and Daniel's mum liked her was a really positive thing; but she couldn't let herself think that this thing between her and Daniel could have a future. He, Jenny and Iain had had a rough time with Jenny's postnatal depression; Daniel didn't need to risk a repeat of all that with another woman who'd suffered badly with depression. So she needed to get her head back in the right place and not let herself dream of what might have been. It wasn't going to happen. The only thing they could offer each other was friendship—and that would have to be enough.

'Iain hasn't stopped talking about your telescope.'

'I'll sort something out so he can come and see it.' Which was being kind to a small child; it had nothing to do with arranging to spend more time with Daniel.

'Won't your family...?' He looked awkward.

'Mind? No. It's fine. Anyway, I guess we need to get on. Patients to see,' she said brightly.

She knew she was being a coward and avoiding him. But she managed to get herself back under enough control during the morning so that for the rest of the week she treated him exactly the same way she treated Josh and Sam and the rest of the team. As a colleague who was becoming a friend, now she'd settled in to her new job. Repeating silently to herself that he was her colleague and nothing but her colleague seemed to be working.

Until Thursday afternoon, when they were both rostered to Resus and she answered a call from the paramedics.

'Hello, Resus. Beatrice speaking.'

'Beatrice, it's Dev Kapoor. We're at an RTC.'

Road traffic collision. That covered a whole range of cases; but, given that he was calling in, it clearly was a more serious one. 'OK. What have you got for us?'

'A guy who may or may not have whiplash and a bump to the head. We're getting another crew out to him, because I'm less worried about him than the other patient: a pregnant woman who's bruised and panicking.'

Beatrice went still. She'd been here before. Nearly five years ago. Except she'd been the one needing the ambulance, not the one on the team treating the patient. With an effort, she got herself back under control and managed to keep her voice steady as she asked, 'How far along is her pregnancy?'

'Twenty-eight weeks,' Dev said.

Oh, God. Twenty-eight weeks. The same as her own had been. But she couldn't afford to think about that now. She needed to compartmentalise it and put her patient's needs first. 'Have you examined her?'

'Yes. Her uterus is woody, and I can't feel

the baby. I'm thinking possible abruption. I've put a line in and put her on oxygen.'

'Good call. I'll talk to the maternity unit and get them on standby. Thanks, Dev. See you when you get here.'

'ETA about ten minutes,' he said.

Everything he'd described sounded like the classic symptoms of placental abruption. A tear in the placenta that pulled it away from the uterine wall. Such a little, little thing.

And it had ripped her life apart.

She took a deep breath. Not now. She needed to get the right specialist support. Support that would hopefully mean this poor woman wouldn't have to go through the same nightmare that Beatrice had struggled through, nearly five years ago.

She called up to the maternity unit. 'Hi, it's Beatrice Lindford from the Emergency Department. Are any of the consultants available? I've got a mum coming in with a suspected abruption.'

'I think I saw Alex Morgan go past a few seconds ago—hang on and I'll try and find him for you,' the midwife who'd answered the phone said.

It felt like for ever, but finally the phone was picked up again.

'Alex Morgan speaking. How can I help?'

'Alex, it's Beatrice from the Emergency Department. I've got a mum coming in with a suspected abruption. She's twenty-eight weeks. Her uterus is woody and the paramedics can't feel the baby. They're bringing her in now; she'll be here in the next ten minutes. I don't know how big the abruption is—whether we'll need to just admit her for monitoring, or whether we'll need to deliver the baby early and get the neonatal special care team involved.'

'I'll call the neonatal team and get them on standby, and I'll come down,' Alex said.

'Thanks. I appreciate it.' She turned to Daniel and filled him in on the situation.

'I'll get the portable scanner,' Daniel said.

'And a Doppler, please,' Beatrice added.

A few minutes later, Dev came in with their patient on a trolley. 'Jessica Rutherford, aged thirty,' he said, and talked them both through the treatment he'd given Jessica on the way.

Jessica was white-faced and clearly panicking.

Beatrice knew how that felt, but strove

to push it behind her. Jessica needed help, and her own emotions just weren't necessary right now. The Lindfords had always managed to keep a stiff upper lip; she was going to follow the family line rather than following her counsellor's advice to talk it through. There was a time and a place.

'Hello, Jessica. I'm Beatrice Lindford and this is Daniel Capaldi, and we're going to be looking after you this afternoon. I've got someone from the maternity team coming down to see you, too. Can you tell us what happened?' she asked.

Jessica took the oxygen mask off so she could talk. 'There was a guy on a motorcycle driving behind me, weaving from side to side and getting a bit too close to me.' Her voice was shaking. 'When he finally overtook me, he was still weaving from side to side—I don't think he was drunk, more like he was young and showing off. I kept my distance, because I had a funny feeling about it, but then he tried to overtake the car in front, misjudged it and had to brake suddenly. I managed to brake and stop before I hit him, but the car behind me didn't stop in time.'

Beatrice knew what that felt like, the shock

of a car crashing into you when you were stationary. Again, she pushed the thought away. Not now. 'I'm sorry you've been through something so scary. Can you tell us how you're feeling, Jessica—any pain anywhere, anything that doesn't feel quite right?'

'My back hurts, but I don't care about that. It's the baby,' Jessica said, the pitch of her voice rising with anxiety. 'I haven't felt him move properly but I don't know if it's because I'm panicking because the guy in the ambulance said he couldn't feel it, or if, if...' She choked on the words.

If her baby hadn't made it.

Beatrice squeezed her hand. 'You're here and we're going to help. Anything else?'

'My bump. It feels tender, like—like a bruise, I guess.'

Beatrice could also see tell-tale bleeding on Jessica's jeans: another likely symptom of an abruption. Jessica didn't appear to be going into shock, so hopefully it was a small abruption rather than a very serious one. Especially as Alex still hadn't arrived from the maternity department. Something had clearly held him up; she really hoped he'd manage to deal with it and get here in the next couple of minutes, or send someone else in his place. 'Daniel, can you get someone to chase Alex up?' she asked.

'Sure,' he said.

'Jessica, I'd like to examine your bump and give you a scan to see what's going on with the baby, if that's all right?'

Jessica's brown eyes were wide with worry. 'Is my baby going to be OK? The paramedics couldn't feel him and he's not moving.'

'You're in pain and your uterus will feel hard in this sort of situation, so it's difficult for them to feel the baby, and as you said you're worried sick so you're thinking the worst,' Beatrice reassured her. 'Let me put the Doppler on—it's a machine that uses sound to pick up your baby's heartbeat and it doesn't hurt. Would you mind pushing your top up for me and pushing the top of your jeans down so I can check the baby's heartbeat? And then I'd like you to put the oxygen mask back on for me.'

Jessica did as she asked, and Beatrice checked for the heartbeat. *Please let it be there. Please don't let this be like what happened to me.*

She only realised that she was holding her

breath when they heard a nice, steady clop-clop: the baby's heartbeat.

'That's sounding good—a nice, steady heartbeat,' she said, smiling at Jessica. 'Did the paramedics call anyone for you?'

Jessica pulled her oxygen mask to one side again. 'Yes. My husband's coming in.'

'Good. I can see there's some blood on your jeans,' Beatrice said, 'but that could be for several reasons, so don't assume the worst. I'm going to do a scan first, and then we'll be able to see if we need to do an internal exam. The scan is identical to the one you had for your dating scan and your twenty-week scan, so you know what to expect. I'm afraid our gel tends to be a bit cold because we don't have all those huge scanners in the room to warm everything up, but it's not going to hurt. If anything does hurt, I want you to tell me straight away, OK?'

'OK,' Jessica said, still looking worried, but the high-pitched edge of panic in her voice had gone.

Daniel came back over. 'Alex has been held up, but someone from the unit will be with us as soon as they can.'

'Thanks,' she said. 'Can you do the gel for me?'

Daniel nodded and squeezed gel onto Jessica's stomach.

Beatrice swept the head of the transponder over Jessica's abdomen; on the screen, she could see the baby clearly and also signs of the abruption. Right at this point, she didn't think the tear was bad enough to warrant an emergency Caesarean section, but she definitely wanted to keep Jessica in overnight for observation in case the situation changed.

She took Jessica's hand. 'OK. I can see everything clearly and I can see what's happened. The baby's looking OK. The reason why your tummy feels as if it's bruised is because there's a little tear in your placenta and part of it has come away from your womb. It's called a placental abruption.'

Jessica looked too shocked and scared to say anything.

'It sounds a lot scarier than it is,' Beatrice said. 'It's actually quite common; around one in a hundred women have a tear in their placenta.'

'Sometimes it happens after an accident, like the one you just had, and sometimes it just happens and nobody knows why,' Daniel added.

'The good news is that I don't think we

need to rush you into Theatre and give you a Caesarean section,' Beatrice reassured her, 'but I do want to admit you to the ward so they can keep an eye on you and the baby, in case the situation changes overnight.'

'And then they'll have to rush me into Theatre and give me a Caesarean?' Jessica dragged in a breath. 'But I'm only twenty-eight weeks. It's too soon for the baby to born. He can't possibly survive.'

'Twenty-eight weeks is early, yes,' Daniel said, 'but if we do have to deliver the baby then he's got a good chance of survival. Neonatal intensive care is really good nowadays.'

Beatrice thought of Taylor, and it was as if someone had punched her hard and taken her breath away. But this situation was different. Taylor hadn't been breathing at all and had no heartbeat; she hadn't stood a chance. This baby had a strong heartbeat and he was fighting.

'Is there something you're not telling me?' Jessica asked, her voice shrill with fear.

'No, not at all,' Beatrice said.

'But, just then, the look on your face...'

Memories. Jessica really didn't need to hear that particular horror story. She needed reassurance. Beatrice squeezed her hand. 'I promise you, there's nothing I'm not telling you. Let me show you so you can see for yourself and relax a bit.' She turned the monitor round so Jessica could see it and swept the scanner head over her abdomen again. 'See? One beating heart, four waving limbs, one baby who's holding his own very nicely right now and is completely oblivious as to how worried his mum is.'

A tear trickled down Jessica's face. 'Thank you,' she whispered. 'I was just so scared that—' her breath hitched '—that the baby would die.'

Beatrice had been there. Except in her case her baby *had* died. 'I know,' she said gently. 'Everything's going to be OK. It's easy for me to say, but try not to worry. We'll keep a really close eye on you both.'

And then, thankfully, Alex came rushing in, full of apologies. Once she'd introduced him to Jessica and filled Alex in on their findings, Alex took over Jessica's care, and Beatrice was able to concentrate on clearing up and checking everything was stocked ready for the next emergency, and doing the routine tasks helped her push the old memories back into place.

* * *

Something was wrong, Daniel thought. He'd seen that look on Beatrice's face, when he'd said that twenty-eight weeks was early but the baby had a good chance of survival. Misery and pain and worry had blurred together. It had been brief, but long enough for their patient to notice, too, and panic that Beatrice was trying to work out how to tell her some bad news.

Right now Beatrice was all brisk and smiling and sorting everything out. But he couldn't shake the feeling that something was wrong. She was a little bit too bright, as if by forcing herself to smile she could lift her mood.

He'd been there himself, when Jenny's postnatal depression had been at its worst. Trying to keep everything together, being bright and brisk and smiling.

The one thing that had helped was talking. And maybe he could do that for Beatrice. Listen to her, as she'd listened to him when he'd explained about Jenny. Dating her, much as he wanted to, wasn't an option—but he could be her friend.

Before they saw their next patient, he called his mother. 'Mum, can you do me a massive favour and pick Iain up from Diane's today?' Thankfully Diane's mother was on the mend from a mini-stroke, so Diane was back in her usual routine of picking Iain up after school.

'Yes, of course,' Susan said. 'Is everything all right?'

'Just busy,' he fibbed, not wanting to share his suspicions about Beatrice even with his mother.

'Leave it to me, love. I'll take him back to yours and give him his tea.'

'Thanks, Mum. I owe you.'

'That's what I'm here for. To support you,' Susan reminded him. 'I didn't do it when you were young, so it's payback.'

'That's all in the past and you've done way more than your fair share, these past five years,' Daniel said. 'And I hope you know you're the best mum and gran in the world.'

'Och, away with you,' Susan said, but the thickening of her accent told Daniel she was pleased.

He caught Beatrice at the end of her shift. 'You and I,' he said, 'are going for a cup of tea.'

She blinked. 'Are we? Why?'

'Resus, this afternoon.'

She spread her hands. 'What about it?'

He recognised the brittleness in her eyes. He'd seen it in Jenny's. 'When our patient said there was something you weren't telling her, I saw it in your face, too.'

Just as he could see the moment of horror in her face now, quickly masked.

'We're friends, Bea,' he said gently.

'Friends,' she echoed.

'I think you need someone to listen to you.'

She shook her head. 'I'm absolutely fine.'

'I've been there,' he said, 'so I don't think you are.' When she said nothing, he added softly, 'Whatever you say to me isn't going to be passed on to anyone else.'

'I…' Her eyes filled with tears, and she blinked them away and wrapped her arms round herself.

'Tea,' he said. 'Not in the hospital canteen. Mum's picking Iain up from Diane, so I have all the time in the world.'

'Let's go to my place,' she said, and there was the tiniest wobble in her voice.

'OK.' He didn't push her to talk on the way, guessing that she needed to get her head together. She let them in, and he followed her into the kitchen.

All the colour had leached from her face, and she looked bereft. 'Sit down,' he said, gesturing to the table in her kitchen. 'Tell me where you keep your tea and I'll make it.'

'The teabags are in the cupboard above the kettle,' she said.

He filled the kettle with water and switched it on, then opened a couple of cupboard doors and retrieved two mugs. Somehow it didn't surprise him that her tea was a fine and delicate Earl Grey. Well, she didn't need fine and delicate right now. She needed strong tea with sugar—even though he knew she usually didn't take sugar. He busied himself making two mugs of tea, added milk to both and sugar to hers.

'Here go you.' He put one of the mugs in front of her, and pulled out the chair opposite hers.

'Thank you.' She took a sip and grimaced. 'Sugar.'

'Simply because you need it right now.'

She didn't protest again, just took another sip and stared into the mug, as if bracing herself. Then she took a deep breath. 'What you told me about Jenny—I've kind of been there.'

Postnatal depression? But as far as he knew she didn't have children.

Kind of. Perhaps not PND, then.

He said nothing, just reached across the table and took her hand. No pressure, no demands: just letting her know that he was here. He didn't push her to talk; from working with his patients, he knew that sometimes you needed space and time until you felt comfortable enough to talk.

And eventually the words came out.

'It was our patient, this afternoon. The one with the abruption.'

He guessed then that it had brought back memories for her. A past patient, or someone close to her?

'That happened to me, nearly five years ago,' she whispered.

An abruption? He went cold as he realised what she was about to tell him. His own personal nightmare was if anything should ever happen to Iain, and no doubt it had been the same for her.

'What happened?' he asked softly, still holding her hand.

'I was in a queue of stationary traffic. I'd had an antenatal appointment that morning and I was driving over to my parents' for lunch.' She blew out a breath. 'It was just an ordinary day. The sun was shining and I was singing along to the radio.'

Just an ordinary day. One, he guessed, that had turned into a nightmare.

'The couple in the car behind me were having a fight. They didn't notice that the traffic had stopped, they crashed into me and pushed my car into the one in front.'

A concertina crash.

The way she was talking about it, it was if she'd detached herself from the situation and was describing it happening to someone else. An impersonal statement of facts. Because sometimes things went so deep, hurt so much, that it was the only way you could deal with them, he thought.

'The airbag didn't go off because I was stationary.' She shrugged. 'Oliver asked about it, but apparently if an airbag goes off when the car isn't moving it can cause more problems than it solves.'

He knew neither of her brothers was called Oliver; presumably Oliver had been her partner, and because she'd told him she was single it was a pretty fair chance the relationship hadn't survived the fallout from the accident.

'I don't remember the steering wheel hitting my abdomen. I think I blacked out for a minute or so. But I knew immediately that something was wrong. I had pain in my back, my abdomen was tender and felt as if I was having contractions. You shouldn't feel even Braxton-Hicks at twenty-eight weeks, let alone real ones.'

Twenty-eight weeks. The same as their patient today. It had taken an incredible amount of courage for Beatrice to deal with the case.

'The ambulance came and the paramedics took me in, but I knew even before I got to the Emergency Department that it was all wrong. It felt wet and sticky between my thighs and I knew it was blood. And I couldn't feel the baby kicking.'

Again, the same as their patient today.

'I was trying not to panic—I knew if the crash had caused an abruption and my uterus was woody, I wouldn't feel any movement, but there'd still be a chance that the baby would make it. A tiny one. That I'd be whipped in for an emergency section and the baby would be in intensive care for weeks, but she'd make it.' She swallowed hard. 'But the doctors couldn't find the baby's heartbeat with the Doppler. They gave me a scan and that's when they said I'd had a severe placental abruption and the baby hadn't survived.'

'I'm so sorry,' he said. 'That's such a hard thing to go through.'

She gave him a grim smile. 'That was the start of it. They had to induce me. I gave birth to a stillborn girl, Taylor.'

He really didn't know what to say, so he just held her hand and let her speak.

'I didn't cope very well. I didn't want to go to work and face everyone's pity, and I really didn't want to be in our house and see the nursery we'd put together for Taylor—even though Oliver's sister was really kind and packed up the nursery for us so we wouldn't have to do it. I went to stay with my parents, because I still couldn't face the house. I knew they wouldn't push me to talk about it, because my family's really not good with talking. They always have a stiff upper lip and pretend everything's fine—even my sisters-in-law are the same.' She lifted one shoulder in a shrug.

'When I saw my doctor, I said everything was fine. But it wasn't. It was like a black hole sucking me in. Nothing felt right and I was totally disconnected from everyone. I suppose the only place I coped was work, because I was too busy to think about what had happened to me. That, and the gym, where I pushed myself harder and harder, doing the kind of training where you count repetitions so you don't have any space in your head to think of anything else. I didn't want to think. I didn't want to remember.'

No wonder she'd understood about Jenny, Daniel thought. She'd been through something very similar herself.

'I kept my lunchbreaks short and I avoided seeing my friends. I avoided Oliver, too. I just didn't want to be with anyone. I got through the days, but that was about all.' She blew out a breath. 'My sister-in-law was due to have George, the same week as Taylor was due. It was so hard to walk into the hospital where I'd lost my baby and visit her, the day George arrived. I couldn't look at Oliver. I felt as if I was drowning, but I couldn't say anything because I didn't want to make them feel bad.'

'Didn't they guess how you were feeling?'

'Probably. But, as I said, my family always pretends everything's just fine and keeps a stiff upper lip. So we never discussed it. And I held that baby and I smiled and said how gorgeous he was, even while my heart was being shredded.' She looked away. 'I love George. But every time I see him, a little bit of me wonders what Taylor would've been doing now.'

Nearly five years ago. A child who would've been four years old. Late summer-born, just like Iain. Was it the same when she saw his son? Daniel wondered. Did she see Iain and think of her lost little girl? She'd been kind and helped him out last week when he'd desperately needed a babysitter. How much had that hurt her? How much had that cost her in unshed tears and pain?

He wanted to hold her and tell her everything was going to be all right, except he knew it wasn't. How did you even begin to come to terms with a loss like that?

'About a month later, I'd got some leave and I was spending it at the castle. And in the middle of that week I just woke up and realised I didn't want to be here any more. I didn't want to be anywhere.' And this time she met his eyes. 'So I took an overdose. Vicky found me—she'd knocked on my door, planning to ask me to go and help feed the ducks with Henry, and when I didn't answer she had a funny feeling and opened my door and saw me lying there with the empty packet of paracetamol beside me.'

An overdose of paracetamol. She'd had to deal with a patient who'd done that, too, very recently. He remembered how the girl's mother had been raging at her selfishness and Beatrice had stuck up for her and explained it was an illness, not done on purpose.

'She called the emergency services, and they patched me up—thankfully not in my own emergency department, because I think that would've been so much worse, facing everyone's pity.' She grimaced. 'When I went back to work, everyone was sympathetic and kind. It just made me feel worse. And then my boss called me into her office. She'd called in a favour from a friend and got me some counselling sessions—and she made me go to them. She took me to the sessions herself; she never asked me anything and never judged me. She just greeted me with a hug when I came out, and took me for coffee and a sandwich, to make sure I ate something healthy.'

'That's really nice,' Daniel said. And it sounded like something Beatrice herself would do, paying it forward.

'The counsellor did a lot for me. She taught me how to talk—something I couldn't do before, and I'm probably talking too much now.'

'You're doing just fine,' he said.

'And she taught me a good grounding exercise.'

'Would it help you to do that now?' he asked.

She nodded. 'You name five things you can see, four things you can hear, three things you can touch, two things you can smell or like the smell of, and take one slow, deep breath. I sometimes do that with my patients if I think it'll help.'

He'd remember that one. 'OK,' he said. 'Tell me five things you can see.'

'The picture Iain drew me from the park. My kitchen table. Two mugs of coffee. The kettle.' She paused and looked him straight in the eye. 'You.'

For a second, he couldn't quite breathe. All he was aware of was Beatrice. 'Four things you can hear,' he prompted, hoping that she wouldn't hear the slight creak in his voice—or, if she did, that she hadn't guessed what had caused it. Now was really *not* the time to have inappropriate thought about her.

'A dog barking. A guitar being played. Waves swishing against a beach. A fairground ride.'

'Three things you can touch.'

'And you touch them. The table. My mug of coffee.' She looked down at their joined hands. 'Your hand.'

Did he let her hand go? Or did he keep holding her hand? He had no idea. All he could do was be guided by Beatrice's actions, and she didn't pull away, so he left his fingers linked with hers.

'Two things you can smell.'

'Coffee,' she said. 'And stocks.'

'Stocks?'

She gestured towards the kitchen windowsill with her free hand. 'My big vice. I love fresh flowers. Especially ones that smell as gorgeous as those stocks.'

A sweet yet spicy fragrance. He could understand why she liked it so much.

'And one deep, slow breath.'

She marked off the seconds with her fingers as she took a slow, deep breath in and out. 'Thank you.'

'It helped?'

'It helped,' she confirmed. 'And thank you for listening.'

'What you've said goes no further than me,' he said. 'And I'm sorry you went through such a terrible experience. Which isn't me pitying you—it's empathy.'

'Because you were in Oliver's shoes. You've been there from the other side. Nothing you can do makes it better, and you feel so helpless and useless. And the wall goes up between you, and you can't talk about it, and all the love just leaks away.'

His fingers tightened around hers. 'And you hate yourself for it, but you can't stop it happening.'

'Are you friends with Jenny now?'

He nodded. 'And I never, ever say anything negative about her in front of Iain. She was good enough to let me have custody. She's remarried and she's happy.'

'Same with Oliver. Well, obviously without the custody issues. But he's remarried and they have a son. I see them occasionally at events.'

Posh events, he guessed, where you smiled and smiled and pretended everything was just fine, no matter how you were feeling.

'It's probably inappropriate,' he said, 'but

what helps me most is a hug. Usually Iain, sometimes my mum. Would a hug help you now?'

Her eyes filled with tears, and she blinked them away. 'You're a kind man.'

'I'm not pitying you,' he said.

She loosened her hand from his hold and stood up. 'A hug would be great.'

He walked round to her side of the table and wrapped his arms round her. She wrapped her arms round him and they stood there together, just holding each other.

She'd been through hell and back. He could understand why she didn't want to get involved with anyone and wanted to concentrate on her career. To lose your child in such an awful way, to lose your marriage... It would be hard to get past the fear that it wouldn't happen all over again. Yes, he and Jenny had had a rough time and their marriage hadn't survived, but they still had Iain and they'd managed to get to the point where they were friends and he was genuinely pleased to see her. For Beatrice, it must be so much harder, seeing her ex with the child they should've had.

He had no idea how long they stood there, just taking comfort from each other's closeness. He dropped a kiss against her hair, wanting to make her feel better. The next thing he knew, they were looking at each other. Her pupils were huge, so her blue eyes looked almost black. Wide and full of longing.

A longing that pulled at him, too.

A shared longing that temporarily took away his sanity, because then he dipped his head and brushed his mouth against hers. Once. Twice. Every nerve-ending in his lips felt as if it had suddenly woken up after years of being asleep.

And then they were really kissing. Hungrily. Desperately. Clinging to each other as if they were drowning in a sea of emotion.

He couldn't remember the last time he'd wanted someone so much. And he was at the point of picking her up and carrying her to her bed when his phone beeped.

The unexpected sound shocked him back to his senses and he pulled back.

'Beatrice. I'm so sorry.'

She looked just as horrified as he did.

'I wasn't hitting on you.' That wasn't strictly true. But he had forgotten himself. Acted on his feelings instead of putting her needs first.

'I know. I…' She shook her head, as if the words just wouldn't come.

He knew how that felt. He was in exactly the same place. He didn't have a clue what to say. 'It was meant to be comfort,' he said. 'Just a hug. Except…' He blew out a breath. Maybe honesty was the best thing he could hope for. 'I haven't felt anything like this about anyone since before Iain was born. I don't actually know what to do right now. Or say.'

'Me, too,' she whispered.

'It was meant to be comfort.'

And it had turned into white-hot desire.

She laid her palm against his cheek. 'I know. And I wasn't…' She grimaced. 'I'm thirty-four years old and I feel like a teenager.'

'So do I.'

'We can't do this.'

'I know.' But it didn't stop him twisting his head so he could press a kiss into her palm. 'In another place and another time, maybe it would be different.'

'We're colleagues.'

'Friends,' he corrected. 'Though I'll try to head Iain off so we don't bother you in future.'

'You don't bother me. He's a sweetheart.'

'You said seeing your nephew brings it back. And Iain's the same age. Surely it's the same situation for you?'

She nodded. 'But you can't have a perfect world. And I'm coming to realise it's better to have a little sadness at the same time as having the pleasure of children around than to avoid them and pretend you're OK.'

'Friends, then,' he said.

'Friends. But I'm not going to kiss your cheek,' she said, 'because it won't stop there. And you need to check your phone. It might be important.'

Reluctantly, he let her go and took the phone from his pocket. 'Mum.' He checked the message. 'She's put Iain to bed.'

'You need to go.'

What she wasn't saying practically echoed between them: *but you could stay...*

Right now, she was vulnerable, and he didn't want to take advantage of her. He was going to follow his head rather than his heart and do the correct thing. Leave, rather than sweep her up in his arms and carry her to her bed. 'I'll see you tomorrow,' he said.

She nodded. 'Thank you for listening.'

'Any time. And that's not me being polite. I'm a Scot. I tell it like it is.'

'Aye, you do,' she said.

He laughed, and retorted with his best attempt at a cut-glass accent, 'That's the worst Glaswegian accent I've ever heard.'

'And the worst posh accent I've ever heard,' she said. 'Thank you, Daniel. For noticing that I was having a wobble, and for making me feel stable again.'

'That's what friends do. Like when you helped me out with Iain.' And how much that must have cost her, he realised now. 'If you can't sleep tonight, call me.'

'I will,' she said, though he knew she wouldn't. 'See you tomorrow.'

CHAPTER SEVEN

BEATRICE HIT THE gym early the next morning, so early that only half a dozen people were there and the punchbag was free.

She'd made such an idiot of herself last night. Spilling her heart out to Daniel, telling him all about the accident and Taylor and her overdose.

He must think she was a basket case.

One good thing might come out of it, though. Last night he would have had time to think about it and realise just how unsuitable she was. That getting involved with her would be risking a repeat of what he had already been through with Jenny—and the most important thing was to keep life stable for Iain. Which meant not getting involved with her.

As for that kiss…

Well, he'd said it last night. In another

place and time, it would have been different; they could have acted on the attraction they'd both admitted to. Taken that kiss further. Much further.

She concentrated on the bag, punching out her frustration.

It wasn't going to happen. They could be colleagues—perhaps friends—and nothing more.

By the time she'd finished her workout, showered and walked into the emergency department, she'd got her mask firmly in place. Beatrice Lindford, Emergency consultant, cool and calm and capable and kind.

That was who she was. Not needy or broken, not the woman who'd let a patient's situation bring back memories, not the woman who'd let her emotions out and felt like a teenager when Daniel Capaldi kissed her.

There wasn't going to be any more kissing.

No more holding each other or holding hands or touching.

Professional. That was the way forward.

Her resolution almost deserted her when she walked into the staff kitchen and saw Daniel there, leaning against the worktop and drinking coffee.

'Hi.'

She was not going to let a pair of dark eyes knock her off course. No matter how sensual they were and no matter how sexy she found Daniel's Scottish accent. The way he rolled his Rs, the way he pronounced world as 'wuruld'—she wasn't going to let it throw her.

And how annoying was it that she could feel the colour rush into her face? Just as well that nobody else was in the kitchen just yet to notice her reaction and join the dots together.

'Hi,' she said.

'Did you sleep OK?' he asked.

No. She'd lain awake until the small hours, thinking of the way her life had imploded and how hard she'd had to work to get it back on track. Thinking of that kiss. Thinking of the way Daniel made her feel. Thinking about how she had to be sensible. 'Yes,' she fibbed.

'Good.' Though his eyes said he didn't quite believe her. 'Tomorrow,' he said, 'Iain is at his mum's. I'm on a late shift. I was thinking, if you're not busy, maybe we could go for a drink or something to eat.'

This was her cue to tell him that, sorry,

she was busy—that she was spending the weekend with her family or something like that. But her mouth wasn't with the programme and she found herself saying, 'I'd like that.'

'Great. I'll pick you up after work,' he said.

Had she just agreed to a date, or was this his idea of being friends? Not that she could ask without feeling like a gauche teenager. 'OK,' she said.

'Good.' And his smile made the whole room feel as if it was filled with sunshine.

That feeling stayed with Beatrice all day, despite her being rostered in Resus and having to face the scene of the case that had affected her so badly yesterday. At the end of her shift, she went up to the maternity unit to see how Jessica Rutherford was doing.

'They're going to let me home tomorrow,' Jessica said, 'on strict condition that I rest.'

So the baby was going to be fine. Relief flooded through her. 'That's so good to hear.'

'And they've been looking after me so well,' Jessica said. 'Thank you—you were all so wonderful yesterday when I was terrified that I'd lose my baby.'

'It's what we're there for,' Beatrice said with a smile. 'I'm glad it's all worked out for you.'

Asking Beatrice out for a drink. When she'd told him all about her past and he knew exactly why she didn't want to get involved with anyone. How stupid was he?

Daniel half expected Beatrice to call it off.

But she didn't. And when she answered the door to him, she was dressed casually, in jeans and a T-shirt, and her glorious blonde curls were loose rather than being tied back, the way she wore her hair at work.

He felt as if his tongue had just stuck to the roof of his mouth and all the words had disappeared out of his head. This behaving like a teenager thing seemed to be becoming a habit when he was around Beatrice Lindford. 'Um, hi.'

'Hi.' She actually blushed. So was it the same for her? And if her marriage had fallen apart at roughly the same time as his own, then like him she probably hadn't dated in years and she'd be just as clueless as he was. And, weirdly, instead of making him feel more awkward, that realisation made him relax.

'So how's your day been?' he asked.

'Very domestic. Cleaning, laundry and grocery shopping. How was yours?'

'Saturday. People coming in, needing to be patched up after a Friday night out when they were so drunk they'd not realised they'd fallen over and hurt themselves until they tried to get out of bed this morning.'

'Ouch.' She grimaced. 'And half of them still had breath that could strip paint, I assume?'

He nodded. 'Plus the gardeners who overdid it and ricked their backs, a few sporting injuries, someone who jumped into a fountain to cool down, slipped over and broke his arm...'

'Usual Saturday stuff, then. Lucky you.' She raised her eyebrows. 'So where are we going?'

'I don't have a clue,' he admitted. 'It's so long since I've been out with anyone other than Iain and my mum, I'm really not there with the cool kids. The only places I know are where the team has a night out, or those indoor play centres with ball pits and slides.'

'I'm not with the cool kids, either—and not just because I don't know the area.' She looked at him. 'We could stay in. Because

I'm on the ground floor, I've got a patio leading off from my living room; and there's a table and chairs. The garden's communal and it's very pretty. We could cook something together to take outside and open a bottle of wine.'

'That,' he said, 'sounds lovely. Except I haven't brought any wine or anything with me.'

She smiled. 'That's not a problem.'

'It is,' he insisted. 'It's imposing on you, expecting you to feed me and give me wine.'

'How are you imposing on me when it was my suggestion?' she pointed out.

He didn't have an answer to that, but the strike wasn't comfortable. 'It isn't the way I was brought up. If we're doing this as friends, then we should go fair shares.' He looked at her. 'If this is a date, then I'm the one to provide everything, because I'm the one who asked you.'

She reached out and took his hand. 'So you're an old-fashioned man, Daniel Capaldi? That's nice. But I'm a very modern woman. If it's a date, I expect to pay my own way. And friends take turns. Maybe if you let me provide the wine and food tonight, you can do it next time.'

So she was already thinking about a next time? That was good. Though he still had no idea if she saw this as a date or as friendship. He wasn't sure which way he saw it, either.

'You're a puzzle, Beatrice Lindford.'

'I'm just me,' she said. 'So would you prefer to go out, or to sit on my patio?'

It had been a long, long day. He just wanted to chill out.

With her.

'The patio,' he said, 'sounds wonderful. Provided you let me help prepare dinner and the washing up is all mine.'

'Deal,' she said.

It had been so long since he'd prepared dinner with someone—apart from alternate Saturday nights with Iain, when his son helped him make the dough and add the toppings to the pizza, but that wasn't quite the same. In the last few months of his marriage, he'd done most of the cooking on his own or bought microwave meals from the supermarket, because Jenny had lost all interest in food. And he'd forgotten how much he enjoyed the domesticity: just pottering about the kitchen with someone.

They divided up the tasks; Beatrice chopped the salad and made the dressing while he grilled mini chicken fillets and warmed through some wholewheat tortillas, and then together they made some make-shift burritos.

'Perfect for summer,' she said. She put on some music while he opened a bottle of dry white wine, and together they took everything out to the patio.

'This is really nice,' he said when they'd finished eating.

'That's why I rented the flat, because it has a patio and a garden,' she said. 'I went to see Jessica Rutherford yesterday at the end of my shift.'

Their patient with an abruption, he remembered. 'How was she?'

'Fine. They're letting her home today, on strict orders to rest. And the baby's doing well.'

'That's good. And it was nice of you to go and see her. Especially as…' He let the words tail off, realising how tactless he was about to be.

'Especially as it was the same thing that happened to me?' She spread her hands. 'Or, let's be honest, the way my counsellor taught me to be. Maybe it was selfish, because I wanted to know that she was OK. That this time there was a good outcome.'

He reached across the table and took her hand. 'Was that the first abruption case you've had to treat since it happened to you?'

'The first one after a car accident, yes.' She gave him a smile tinged with sadness. 'I hope the other driver in the accident knows she's OK.'

'Did the one who crashed into you know what happened?'

She nodded. 'He felt terrible about it. So did his wife. The police were going to prosecute him for driving without due care and attention, but taking him to court and giving him a fine and getting his licence endorsed wasn't going to bring Taylor back. There was nothing anyone could do to make it better. I just had to come to terms with the situation.'

'Have you?' he asked gently.

'Yes. I get the occasional bad day, but most of the time I'm OK.' She looked at him. 'But that's why I haven't dated anyone since I split up with Oliver. Because I don't think I can handle the risk of another abruption and losing a baby again. I know intellectually that the chances are I'll be perfectly fine— the abruption was caused by an accident, and thankfully I've not been in many—but emotionally I just can't do it.'

'I understand,' he said. 'It's one of the reasons I haven't dated again since Jenny and I split up. Even if I found someone who can love Iain as much as I do and will stick around, what if she wants a baby and what if she ends up with postnatal depression as severe as Jenny had?' He blew out a breath. 'Like you, intellectually I know the stats, but actually taking that risk…' He shook his head with a grimace.

'Given what I did after I lost Taylor, I'm just about the worst person you could get involved with,' she said.

'On paper, you're probably right,' he said, knowing how cruel it sounded—but this was important. Important enough that only brutal honestly had any place here.

'And on paper you're the worst person I could get involved with. A man whose child is the same age my little girl would've been. A constant reminder of what I've lost,' she said.

Equally brutal, but true.

So now they were both clear what was standing in the way.

'Except,' he said, 'you're the first person who's made me feel anything since Jenny.'

'And you're the first person who's made me feel anything since Oliver,' she said.

So it was the same for her. This crazy pull of attraction that really shouldn't work. 'Where does this leave us?' he asked. 'Do we just ignore how we feel and try to look at each other as strictly a colleague?'

She looked at their joined hands. 'Whenever I see you outside work, it makes me feel like a teenager.'

'Me, too,' he admitted. 'Thirty-four going on seventeen.'

'So we're going to have to do something.' She paused. 'Get it out of our systems, perhaps?'

He hadn't expected her to suggest that. 'A fling?'

'I don't know. Maybe I don't mean a fling, Maybe more seeing where this takes us.' She looked at him. 'Which means, as far as Iain's concerned, we're just friends who work together.'

So if it went wrong between them, Iain wouldn't be collateral damage. He wouldn't be hurt. Wouldn't feel abandoned. 'Thank you for putting him first,' Daniel said. 'I appreciate that.'

'It's how I'd feel if I were in your shoes.'

Putting himself in her shoes was much harder. 'Are you sure you can cope with seeing Iain?' he asked. If he'd lost his precious boy, it would rip him to shreds every time he came into contact with a child who would've been Iain's age.

'As I said, I have good days and bad days. And he's a total sweetheart. I enjoyed having him here.' She sucked in a breath. 'But I don't want you to think that I'm just using you to get the child I should've had.'

'No, I don't think that. I think it's going to be complicated,' he said, 'but I also think it's going to be worth it.'

'So this is a date?' she checked.

'I think it is,' he said.

'And, right now, there's something I really want to do.' Still keeping his hand linked with hers, he stood up. 'Would you dance with me?'

She'd been more honest with Daniel than she had with Oliver; her time in counselling had taught her how to open up properly and really talk about a situation, rather than burying her emotions under a smile and pretending everything was just fine. Oliver hadn't been able to cope with the depth of her pain, shying away from the emotion.

But Daniel was different. He, too, had had life implode around him. He'd been just as honest with her about his doubts as she'd been with him about her worries.

This was going to be a new start for both of them.

No promises of what the future would hold: which meant that everything was wide open. They could crash and burn, or they could find new strength and new joy in each other.

It had been a long time since she'd felt that sudden surge of possibilities.

'I'd like that.' She stood up and walked into his arms.

She couldn't remember the last time she'd danced with someone. Oliver, probably, at a wedding or something. Years ago. But it felt right to be in Daniel's arms.

'OK?' he asked.

'Very OK. Right now I feel as if I'm floating on air,' she said.

'Me, too.' He drew her close and they

swayed together in the late evening sunshine, cheek to cheek.

She wasn't sure which of them moved first, but then they were kissing. The softest, sweetest kiss that started out making her feel all warm and cherished and wanted; and then it was like lighting touch paper and desire flared though her.

Daniel clearly felt it, too, because when he broke the kiss he looked dazed.

'Beatrice, I…'

'Me, too,' she said.

His eyes were full of longing. 'Right now, I'd really like to carry you to your bed. But I don't have anything with me.'

Meaning he hadn't automatically expected her to have sex with him tonight, even though this evening had been sort of a date. She liked that. 'I don't have anything, either,' she admitted.

'We can't take risks.'

'Absolutely,' she agreed.

'Let's take a rain check,' he said. 'I'm going to do your washing up, and then I'm going home, because you tempt me beyond anything I've felt in years, and that isn't fair to either of us.'

'Rain check,' she said. 'And maybe we'll

be better prepared another time.' That wasn't a maybe. It was a definite. Because she was going to buy contraceptives for the first time in years.

He stroked her face. 'Another time. A night when Iain's at his mum's, so we'll have all the time we want. No pressure, no expectations.'

She could hardly believe she was actually *planning* to have sex with Daniel Capaldi. But neither of them wanted an accidental baby, so this was being sensible. Acknowledging the attraction and the fact that they both wanted to do something about it.

'That sounds good,' she said. And her voice *would* have to croak.

'I'm going to do the washing up, then leave you in peace,' he said.

'Maybe I'll let you off washing up duties,' she said. 'On the grounds that the longer we're together, the less likely we are to be sensible.'

He stole a kiss. 'You're probably right. I'm on a late, tomorrow, how do you fancy a walk in the park? We'll be in public so we'll be sensible And I'll buy you a coffee and a bacon sandwich in the café.'

'That,' she said, 'sounds perfect.'

'Half-past nine at the boating lake,' he said. 'The views over the city are amazing.'

'Half-past nine at the boating lake,' she agreed.

The kiss goodbye he gave her at her front door made her feel as if her knees were melting.

And the kiss hello he gave her at the boating lake, the next morning, had exactly the same effect.

'Well, hello.' He stroked her face. 'I'm glad you didn't change your mind overnight.'

'I thought about it,' she admitted. 'We've both got a lot of baggage.'

'So we know to be careful with each other. No pity and no pressure,' he said. 'And maybe we both deserve a second chance.'

'Agreed.' She looked at him. 'This is scary. But, at the same time, being with you makes it feel as if someone turned the brightness up.'

'Same here,' he said, and took her hand. 'I promised you views. Let's walk up here by Alexandra Palace.'

She gasped when they stopped at the edge of the hill and looked over the railing. 'That's stunning. That's the whole of the City.'

'I hoped you'd like it.'

They headed down to the park, which seemed to be full of dog-walkers and families out playing ball, but instead of thinking about the might-have-beens, this time Beatrice focused on just enjoying the here and now. The sunshine, fresh air, gorgeous scenery—and the equally gorgeous man holding her hand.

She noticed two collies streaking across the park; then the dogs came over to her and Daniel and circled them.

'I think we're being herded,' she said with a grin.

'What?'

'Look.' She pointed to the collies. One of them was lying down, watching them closely and keeping his yellow eyes trained on them. 'If he was human, he'd be playing a character like one of Robert de Niro's, pointing his index and middle fingers at his eyes and then his index finger at us,' she said.

'Seriously?' Daniel asked.

'I dare you to move,' she said, indicating the other collie, which was standing watching them, 'because that one's waiting to round us up.'

Daniel took three steps to the side, and the collie moved towards him.

'See? He wants you to stay put.' She crouched down and extended one hand. 'Come on, boy. I think you're meant to be playing, not working.'

The collie moved towards her and sniffed her hand, just as its owner came puffing up, looking apologetic.

'I'm so sorry,' she said. 'They don't mean any harm.'

'Just their working instinct kicking in,' Beatrice said with a smile. 'We used to have sheep when I was younger, and the collies used to round up all the children in the garden whenever we had people over on a Sunday afternoon. They used to round up the cats as well.'

The woman smiled and looked slightly less embarrassed. 'Thank you for being so understanding. They can be a bit intimidating. I thought that by having two they'd be company for each other and they'd play together, but instead they just go into herding mode.'

Daniel smiled. 'Well, it's the first time I've ever been herded.'

Once the collies had trotted off with their owner, he looked at Beatrice. 'So you're a dog person?'

'Yes. We've always had dogs at Beresford. I would've liked a dog of my own, a liver and white English springer spaniel, but you know the hours junior doctors work, and Oliver worked long hours, too.' It had been part of her dreams: a baby and then a dog, taking them both out to the park and playing endless games of fetch. But her life was a different shape now. It wasn't going to happen.

'I like dogs,' Daniel said, 'but I never grew up with them. My grandparents worked really long hours so it wasn't practical. We had a ginger cat—I got to name him when I was tiny, so he was called Mr Marmalade—but you can't take a cat for a run in the park.'

'We had cats, too. And in our kitchen you'd find an orphan lamb or two every spring—we'd take turns in bottle-feeding them.' She wrinkled her nose. 'We don't have a big flock any more, though. Sandy's in charge of the farming side now and he's part way through turning it into a rare breeds farm park so he can do something about conservation. We've got Hereford cattle and those big woolly Highland cattle with the long horns, and we've got Soay sheep and Jacobs. And every single one of them has a name.'

'It sounds amazing. Iain loves that sort of thing.'

'He could come and help feed them,' she said.

'We'd both like that.' He looked at her. 'So if your middle brother's in charge of the farming side, is your oldest brother in charge of the castle?'

'That, and learning the ropes from Daddy.'

'Are you sure your dad isn't a prince?' he asked.

His tone was light, but she could tell that he was worried about her background. 'No. He's a viscount—which isn't as grand as it sounds. In peerage terms, that's the fourth rank; it's below an earl, who in turn is below a marquess, who in turn is below a duke. And then you have the Queen.'

'So I'd call your dad Viscount Lindford?'

'Lord Lindford,' she said. 'But he'd probably tell you to call him Edward.'

'Does that mean you're Lady Lindford?'

'No, that's Mummy. My brothers and I have a courtesy title—we're all Hons—but don't worry. My brothers aren't stuffy in the slightest. You'd get on well with them.' She smiled. 'I love my family to bits, but they're hopeless at talking about wobbly stuff. As soon as conversations start to get a bit deep or awkward, they get changed to something bright and breezy. I'm the only one of us who doesn't do that—and that's only because I've learned how to discuss things from working with patients and from exercises my counsellor did with me.'

'Uh-huh,' he said.

She decided to ask him outright. 'Does my background worry you?'

'Sort of,' he said. 'Your family sounds so much grander than mine. You can probably trace your ancestors back to William the Conqueror, and I've never even met my father. His name isn't on my birth certificate.'

He really thought that would matter to her? 'Firstly,' she said, 'we don't go back as far as William the Conqueror. The first Viscount Lindford was created by Charles II, and the family story is that's because his wife was one of Charles's favourite actresses. Secondly, there's a bit of a question mark over who was the second Viscount Lindford's dad—it might have been the first viscount, or it might have been Charles, or it might have been another actor from Lizzie's troupe. So don't ever think that your background would make the slightest difference to me or to my family. It's *you* who matters.'

'Thank you. And I'm sorry for—well.' He looked awkward.

'Thinking I might be a snob?'

'Thinking it might matter.'

'It doesn't. And, at the risk of behaving like my family and avoiding wobbly stuff, I think we'd better go and get that bacon sandwich,' she said, 'or you're going to be late for your shift.'

CHAPTER EIGHT

OVER THE NEXT couple of weeks, Beatrice and Daniel snatched as much time as they could together. Not at work—neither of them wanted to be the hot topic on the hospital's gossip grapevine—but if they were both on a late shift they'd meet for breakfast in a café after Daniel had dropped Iain at school, or they'd stroll through the park and grab a bacon roll from the kiosk there, or Beatrice would make eggs Florentine or smoked salmon and cream cheese bagels and they'd eat breakfast on her patio, teamed with strong Italian coffee. And in the evenings, after Iain had gone to bed, Daniel videocalled her and they talked for hours about life, death and the universe.

Beatrice was finding Daniel harder and harder to resist. At work, whenever she caught his eye and he smiled at her, it made her knees go weak. Remembering what it felt like to be in his arms—what it felt like to kiss him. And she really liked the man he was: clever, capable and kind.

And, even though part of her was wary about taking their relationship to the next stage, a greater part of her found it more and more difficult to stop at just kissing.

On Friday night, Daniel video-called her as usual.

'Iain's at Jenny's tomorrow,' he said casually.

Her heart skipped a beat. 'What shift are you on?'

'Early.' He paused. 'And I've a day off on Sunday.'

Meaning they could have the whole night and day together—because her off-duty just happened to dovetail with his.

'What did you have in mind?' she asked carefully, aware that her heart rate had just sped up a couple of notches.

'I don't have to be home early.'

'Or at all.' The words slipped out before she could stop them.

'Are you saying…?' He paused.

Crunch time. He was giving her the choice. She could back away—or she could be brave and reach out for what she wanted. She took a deep breath. 'You could,' she said, 'stay. I have a spare unused toothbrush.'

'A spare unused toothbrush,' he repeated.

'And a washing machine.' So she could put his clothes through it quickly that night and they'd be dry by morning. And he wouldn't need pyjamas.

'So we could go out somewhere. A proper date. Dinner or dancing or something. And then...'

The sensual expression in his eyes was obvious, even on a tablet screen. It sent her pulse rate even higher. 'And then,' she whispered.

'Think about where you'd like to go and text me,' he said. 'And I'll pick you up tomorrow after my shift.'

She thought about it for the rest of the evening.

Were they rushing this, making a mistake?

Or was it better to seize the chance of happiness when you found it?

The next morning, she texted Daniel.

How about an early showing at one of the cinemas in the West End, then dinner out?

He texted back.

Sounds great. You pick the film and I'll organise dinner. Somewhere near Leicester Square?

Perfect, she said.

They'd talked enough for her to know that they both liked good drama. She found a film she thought they'd enjoy and booked the tickets online, then texted him with the show times. And although she normally spent her day off catching up with laundry and domestic chores, she found it hard to concentrate.

An official date.

A movie and dinner.

And Daniel was going to stay the night.

Her breath caught. Oh, for pity's sake. Anyone would think she was seventeen, not a thirty-four-year-old senior doctor. But she was nervous and excited in equal parts, like a teenager on her first date.

Though there was one essential bit of shopping she needed. Hoping that she wasn't going to bump into anyone from work—or at least that she could hide the condoms in her basket by covering them with a large slab of chocolate—she headed to the supermarket.

* * *

When Daniel rang her doorbell later that afternoon, she was a bundle of nerves.

'Hi.' He presented her with practically an armful of sweet-scented stocks, her favourite flowers.

'They're gorgeous. Thank you.' And he looked gorgeous, too, dressed up for a night out. She was glad she'd made the effort with a pretty summer dress and strappy sandals; Daniel was tall enough for her to be able to wear high heels and not tower over him. 'I'll put them in water.'

'I brought this as well. Which doesn't have to be for tonight, and there aren't any strings attached to it.' He handed her a carrier bag.

She looked inside. 'Champagne?'

'English sparkling wine. It has good reviews.'

'It looks lovely. Thank you. I'll put that in the fridge.'

He followed her into the kitchen and kissed her lingeringly. 'You look beautiful.'

'So do you.'

'Men can be beautiful?'

'Aye, ye big, sleekit…'

'Tim'rous beastie?' He exaggerated his accent deliberately. 'I hate to tell you this, but

Rabbie Burns was describing a mouse. And I might be holding back at the moment, but I'm no mouse.'

No. He was all man. Heat shot through her.

'I might even be a troglodyte,' he said, and twirled the very ends of her hair round his fingers. 'I love your hair like this.'

This was getting dangerously close to wobbly talk. She took refuge in the way her family normally did things, and changed the subject. 'Good shift?'

'Typical Saturday. Made much better for the fact that I'm seeing you tonight.' He stole another kiss. 'We have a date. Much as you tempt me to switch this to a night in, I think anticipation is going to make this all the sweeter.'

'What if I disappoint you?' The words were out before she could stop them.

'You're not going to disappoint me.' He stroked her face and smiled. 'It's not going to be perfect. We're on a learning curve until we find out what each other likes. But it's going to be fun finding out.'

And suddenly that took all her worries away so, like him, she could look forward to tonight with anticipation rather than nervousness.

It was a long, long time since she'd held hands with anyone in a cinema. Or sat with their arm round her shoulders. And she thoroughly enjoyed the film; more than that, she enjoyed dissecting the film with Daniel over dinner.

He'd picked a restaurant just off Covent Garden that she'd never been to before, but she loved the way the room was lit by strings of fairy lights threaded through the branches of bay trees dotted between the tables, and there were tea lights in glass and ironwork lanterns that turned the candlelight into shapes of stars.

'This is so romantic,' she said. 'I didn't even know this place was here. How did you find it?'

'Seriously?'

'Seriously.'

He laughed. 'I looked up "romantic restaurants near Leicester Square" on the Internet.'

She liked the fact that he'd admitted it rather than trying to feed her a line about knowing all the best places to go in the city. 'Good find.'

'The reviews all said the food was as good as it looks, so I thought it was worth a try. Luckily they'd just had a cancellation so I was able to get us a table,' he said.

And it was fabulous. A sharing platter of *meze*—baked feta cheese, bread, olives, taramasalata and stuffed vine leaves— followed by lemon chicken with rosemary potatoes, spinach and honey-roasted tomatoes, and then a selection of tiny sweet Greek pastries served with bitter coffee. He ordered a bottle of sparkling wine to go with it—the Greek answer to champagne—and everything was absolutely perfect. The food, the wine, the conversation, the company.

'I've had a wonderful time tonight,' she said when he walked her home from the tube station and they stood outside her front door.

'Me, too.' He took her hand. 'No pressure. If you want me to go home right now, that's fine.'

'Do you want to go home?' she asked.

'No. But this is all new. We don't have to do anything you're not comfortable with. I could sleep on your sofa.'

'No. I want you to stay. And not on my

sofa,' she said, feeling the colour bloom in her face.

'I'm glad,' he said softly. 'But if you should change your mind at any point, that's OK.'

She took a deep breath. 'Let's be brave. Take a risk on each other—but that's the *only* risk,' she added as she unlocked the door.

He followed her inside. 'Great minds think alike. I went to the supermarket yesterday.'

'So did I,' she said. 'So let's open that fizz.'

'And as I didn't get to dance with you earlier…'

'You do the wine and I'll do the music,' she said. Teamwork. It was how they functioned at work. Home wasn't so very different.

'Deal. Where do you keep your glasses?' he asked.

'Top of the cupboard next to the kettle.'

She connected her phone to the speaker, flicked into her music app and chose a playlist of slow dances.

He handed her a glass. 'To us. And to second chances.'

'To us, and second chances,' she echoed,

and took a sip of wine before placing her glass on the kitchen table.

He held out his arms and she walked over to him.

'This is perfect,' he said, 'for dancing cheek to cheek.'

She closed her eyes and swayed to the music with him. And it felt so right when he kissed the corner of her mouth. She turned her head slightly so that he could kiss her properly.

Daniel and the music and the last vestiges of the sunset spilling in through the kitchen window—this was perfect, she thought.

And when he broke the kiss and looked at her, his sensual dark eyes filled with a question, there was only one answer. 'Yes.'

His smile was sweet and slow and sexy as hell. 'Forgive me for being a troglodyte.' And then he scooped her into his arms.

'You're carrying me to my bed?' she asked.

'That's the idea. Like a chieftain carrying his lass off to his lair. Except it's your lair rather than mine,' he said with a grin.

Desire flooded through her. 'Out of the kitchen, second door on the right,' she said.

And he carried her to her bed.

* * *

The next morning, Beatrice woke feeling warm and comfortable, with Daniel's arms wrapped round her.

'Good morning,' he whispered against her hair.

'Good morning.' She twisted around to face him. Funny, she'd thought she might feel shy with him, this morning. Yet this felt real and natural and right. A slow, easy Sunday morning.

'What do you want to do today?' he asked.

'I don't mind, as long as I'm with you,' she said.

'I have to pick up Iain from Jenny's at four,' he said.

And she knew he meant on his own. Which was fine by her, because she, too, thought they needed time to be sure where this was going before they told anyone, especially someone who was so young and could be so badly hurt by the fallout if anything went wrong. 'That's fine.' She paused. 'We could go out for the day. Maybe to Notting Hill and browse in the antique shops and then have lunch in a café somewhere—I know we won't get the market stalls on Portobello

Road, with it being a Sunday, but it could still be fun.'

'Notting Hill.'

She smiled. 'That's one of my favourite films, actually. I love Hugh Grant. We could go location-spotting and find the little square where he kisses Julia Roberts.'

'Kissing,' he said thoughtfully. 'You had me at kissing...'

It was a lot later by the time they finally got up. And they held hands all the way on the tube to Notting Hill, all the way down Portobello Road, and all the way to the little private gardens used in the film. 'You can't go in there because it's locked,' Beatrice said, 'but this is definitely the place.'

'So how exactly did you know where this was?' Daniel asked.

'My sisters-in-law agree with me that it's the best romcom ever. We had a girly weekend in London when I qualified as a doctor,' she said. 'A *Notting Hill* weekend. We went location-spotting—Portobello Road, the bookshop, the flat with the blue door, the restaurant and the cinema. And then we had afternoon tea at the Ritz, and we went back to my flat for pizza and bubbles and we watched *Notting Hill* twice.'

'Twice?'

'It's a girl thing,' she said with a grin. 'My brothers thought we were crackers, but we had a ball. I think I might even have a couple of the pictures still on my phone.' She flicked through. 'There you go. Us with the blue door, the bookshop, and here at the gardens.'

He looked at the photographs. Three young women, with their arms round each other and the broadest smiles.

'So you're close to your sisters-in-law?' He knew how stupid the question was as soon as it left his lips—from those smiles, they were clearly very close indeed.

But she didn't seem to mind. 'Like my brothers, they can't talk about wobbly stuff, but they'll be the first with cake and a hug and then a very awkward pat on the back.' She smiled. 'I love them dearly.'

'*Notting Hill*.' He wasn't entirely sure he'd seen the film—as far as he was concerned, a lot of the romcoms blended into each other—but she'd mentioned that this place involved kissing. 'Then I think a selfie is in order,' he said, and took out his phone to snap them standing by the entrance gate with their arms round each other. 'And a kiss.'

'I thought you'd never ask,' she said, and kissed him.

And his mouth tingled for the next ten minutes.

It was a fun, frothy and light-hearted afternoon and, even though he'd never thought of himself as the sort who'd poke about in an antique shop, he thoroughly enjoyed being with Beatrice.

'Oh, perfect,' she said softly as they browsed in one shop.

'What?'

'Vicky collects those Staffordshire mantel dogs,' she said, gesturing to a pair of stylised china dogs. 'It's her birthday next month. And that's a nice-looking pair.'

'Are you sure? They don't look like a pair. I mean, the decorations are different,' Daniel said.

'Which is one of the ways you can tell they're antique and not reproduction,' she said. She picked one up and looked at it. 'And, look, there are fine brush-stroke details of the dog's hair, the gold isn't shiny and doesn't reflect things, and there's paint on the back.' She looked at the base. 'And no casting holes—this is a press mould, not slipware.'

He coughed. 'If I hadn't seen you treat patients for myself, I'd be wondering if you were an antiques expert rather than a doctor.'

She grinned. 'This is all stuff Vicky taught me. I bought her a pair for Christmas one year and they turned out to be reproductions—and I'd paid well over the odds for them. She showed me what to look for and I've got a much better idea of value, too. She'd love these. I'm going to haggle.'

'This is a shop, not a market stall. You can't haggle!' Daniel said, scandalised.

'Yes, I can.' She went over to the cash desk, and he followed in her wake.

Beatrice was utterly, utterly charming.

And she was a hard negotiator. By the time she'd finished, she'd knocked twenty-five per cent off the price, and the man in the shop had offered them both very good coffee and expensive biscuits while he wrapped the Staffordshire dogs carefully.

'You,' Daniel said when they left the shop, 'are amazing.'

She gave him a sketchy bow. 'Thank you.'

'And this has been such fun.'

She glanced at her watch. 'But you need

to go. Iain's expecting you, and if you're late he'll want to know why.' She kissed him. 'Go.'

'I should see you home.'

She shook her head. 'I'm fine. And I'm going to call Vicky and get her to meet me off the train so I can give her these. Thank you for the weekend. It's been...'

'Amazing,' he said softly, and kissed her lingeringly. 'If you're sure, then I'll see you tomorrow.'

Over the next fortnight, they managed to snatch some time together—including a Friday evening at a departmental pub quiz where Beatrice's more unusual general knowledge meant that the Emergency Department won, to the delight of the rest of the team.

But Daniel was reflective on the Monday evening—Iain had gone to a friend's after school, so he and Beatrice had grabbed the chance to spend some time together.

'Are you going to tell me what's wrong, or would you prefer me to pretend I haven't noticed that you're brooding?' she asked.

He blew out a breath. 'Sorry.'

'Don't apologise. If you want a listening ear, I'm here. If you don't, no offence taken.'

He took her hand and pressed a kiss into her palm. 'It's not the most tactful subject.'

'I'm still listening.'

He sighed. 'Jenny told me last night that she and Jordan are expecting. She's just had her twelve-week scan.'

A baby.

'Has she told Iain yet?'

'No. She said she wanted to talk it over with me, first, and work out the best way to tell him.'

She didn't think it was the baby that was worrying him. She could just pretend that everything was fine and be bright and breezy; or she could be open and honest, and let him talk about his real feelings. 'And you're worried she's going to get postnatal depression again?'

He nodded. 'You know as well as I do, statistically there's an increased risk of having postnatal depression again if you've had it before.'

'But,' she said, 'forewarned is forearmed. As long as her family doctor and her midwife know, they can monitor her and help her if they think she's showing any signs. There are support groups, too. She can get help beforehand and make sure she gets plenty of rest afterwards—and exercise, because the endorphins are really good at helping.'

'Is that what you'd do?' he asked.

Put things in place so she wouldn't end up being depressed after the baby's birth, remembering Taylor? There was just one tiny thing that would affect that plan. 'I don't intend to have any more children,' she said. 'But, hypothetically speaking, if I was in Jenny's situation that's what I'd do. I'd make sure I had counselling during the pregnancy and enough support during the pregnancy and afterwards. If she needs antidepressants, then the doctor can give them sooner rather than later, to make sure she doesn't hit the same low she had last time round.' She looked at him. 'I assume that's what you said to her?'

He grimaced. 'I might need to apologise and buy her flowers and tell her she'll have support from me, from Mum and from Iain as well as from Jordan and his family.'

'You actually told her you were worried she'd have postnatal depression again?'

'I was thinking of Iain. I should've considered her.' He sighed. 'I need to call her, don't I?'

'Do it now,' Beatrice said. 'I'll hang around in the kitchen and make us a pot of tea, and you can call her from the garden or the sitting room, whichever's more comfortable for you. Come and get your tea when you've talked to her.'

She was halfway through her own mug of tea when Daniel returned to the kitchen and wrapped his arms round her. 'You're a good woman and I don't deserve you. That's a quote from Jenny, by the way.'

'You told her about us?'

'In strictest confidence. I think I owed her honesty, when I was a bit too honest with her yesterday,' he said. 'She wanted to know what caused my sea-change in attitude.'

'I see,' she said.

'I told her we weren't ready to say anything to Iain yet, because we wanted to be sure and not let him get hurt. She understands. She said to thank you for the advice, that you're a better doctor than me, and she owes you lunch.'

'Because she wants to check me out?' Beatrice asked.

He wrinkled his nose. 'Iain's already told

her about you—oh, and by the way, I explained that you don't know Prince Harry so he won't be having lunch with you both—and I said that Mum likes you. Which she says is fine, but she'd still like to have lunch with you.'

Beatrice smiled. 'It's nice that she's still looking out for you. And you're still looking out for her—otherwise you wouldn't be so worried about her having postnatal depression again.'

'I'm still worried,' he admitted. 'And Iain's old enough now to notice what's going on. What if she does get it again, and it reminds her of the first time round, and she rejects him?'

'She's his mum. She won't reject him. I'm sure she'll talk to him about being an older brother and being able to boss his little brother or sister around. And I'm the youngest of three, so I can back her up,' Beatrice said.

Daniel hugged her. 'You're a good woman.'
She smiled. 'I try.'

Almost two weeks later, Jenny still hadn't told Iain about his little brother or sister to be, but she'd arranged to take him to the seaside for the weekend, picking him up from school on the Friday afternoon. Both Beatrice and Daniel managed to arrange getting Friday off as well as the weekend.

'I think we can go to the seaside, too,' Daniel said. 'Except obviously not the same place. I was thinking Cornwall.'

'Good choice,' Beatrice said. 'Miles of sand, *Poldark* and good fish restaurants. Cornwall would be wonderful.'

Except when she got up on Friday morning, ready to pack, she felt odd. Queasy.

She hadn't eaten anything unusual, or anything that might've made her feel that way.

And her breasts felt tender.

The last time she'd felt like this, she'd been pregnant with Taylor…

She shook herself. This was utterly ridiculous. Of course she wasn't pregnant. She couldn't be. She and Daniel had been supercareful about contraception. Neither of them wanted a baby.

But the nagging feeling wouldn't leave her, all the way through packing.

'Don't be so *feeble*, Beatrice Lindford,' she admonished herself out loud. 'You know perfectly well that you can practically set your calendar by your menstrual cycle. More regular than clockwork. Your next one's due...'

She went still.

Her next period was due in two weeks' time. Meaning that *her last period had been due two weeks ago.*

She counted it up in her head again. And then on a physical calendar, just to make sure.

Two weeks late.

She went into the bathroom and splashed her face with water. Her period was late. That didn't necessarily mean that she was pregnant. There were all kinds of reasons why your period could be late or you'd miss one. A hormonal imbalance, for starters— though she knew that wasn't likely, and she could discount thyroid issues or polycystic ovary syndrome, too. Ditto the menopause, diabetes or coeliac disease. She could cross off doing extreme exercise and suffering from an eating disorder, too, and her body weight was smack in the middle of the normal range for her height. She hadn't just started the Pill, so her body didn't need to adjust to that.

Maybe it was because she'd started her

new relationship with Daniel. Even though she was happy and enjoying it, subconsciously she could be worrying and the stress had affected her cycle.

Though the fact that she was mentally going through every single medical reason—except the most likely—was telling in itself, she thought grimly. She and Daniel had been careful about contraception to the point of being paranoid, but there was only one method that was one hundred per cent guaranteed. Abstinence. A method they most definitely hadn't used.

There was only one way to settle things. And there was no way she could go to Cornwall with Daniel for a long weekend without knowing the truth. She glanced at her watch. She had an hour until he was due to pick her up. Which gave her enough time to nip out to the supermarket, buy a pregnancy test and use it.

She downed a large glass of water, then headed out. Actually going to the shop and buying the test was a blur. But then she was in her bathroom, doing the test. Peeing on the stick. Waiting for the test to work.

The last time she'd done this, she'd waited so hopefully and happily, praying that it would be positive. She'd been thrilled to see the second line on the screen, a nice clear stripe that said she was definitely pregnant. She'd cried with joy when she'd walked out of the bathroom to tell Oliver the news.

This time, she was filled with panic. She couldn't be pregnant. She and Daniel were still in the early stages of their relationship. Daniel had Iain to think about. And her pregnancy last time had ended in utter heartbreak. Yes, people said that lightning didn't strike twice, but it did. There were trees on the estate back at Beresford that been hit three times. Supposed it happened again? What if she was involved in another car accident that meant her bump hit the steering wheel and caused an abruption? What if she had a spontaneous abruption? *What if? What if?*

The panic spiralled tighter in her head.

One line. The test was working.

Please don't let there be a second. Please.

This was the only test they'd had in the nearest shop. An old-fashioned one. Why hadn't she gone somewhere else and bought a different one, the sort that actually said the word *pregnant* in clear letters so there could be no doubt about it, no possibility that the line was so faint she could kid herself it wasn't there?

She squeezed her eyes tightly shut. Please let the test be negative. *Please*.

And what if it was positive? How would Daniel react? Two weeks ago, he'd reacted badly to Jenny's news, worrying that she would have postnatal depression again and Iain would get hurt. With Beatrice's own history of mental health, there was a high chance that she would be affected by post-natal depression. Daniel's worst nightmare, repeated all over again.

He was a good man. She knew he'd try his best to support her.

But if it was a question of supporting her or protecting Iain, there was only one choice he could make. Walk away.

She wrapped her arms round herself, shivering despite the warmth of the day. Right now, she was panicking too much to think clearly. She couldn't answer any of her own questions; all she could do was worry. Wait. Rinse and repeat.

She opened her eyes and stared at the test.

Two lines.

Positive.

She was pregnant.

What the hell was she going to do?

She couldn't go to Cornwall with Daniel today, that much was clear. OK, so she knew the truth now, but she needed time to process it. To work out how she felt, what she wanted to do—and how she was going to break the news to Daniel.

She glanced at her watch.

Half an hour until he was due to pick her up.

That wasn't enough time for her to get her head together. She needed space. And there was only one place she wanted to be right now.

She was already packed for the weekend, so all she had to do was to lock her front door and sling her bag in the back of her car.

And then she sat in the driver's seat with the engine still turned off and her mobile phone in her hand.

Knowing she was being an utter coward, but unable to think clearly enough to find a better solution, panicking as the seconds ticked by faster and faster, she tapped out a text to Daniel.

Sorry. Can't make Cornwall. Will call you later.

She pressed 'send', then switched off her phone, turned the key in the ignition, and drove away.

CHAPTER NINE

'BYE, DARLING. HAVE a lovely time at the seaside with Mummy and Jordan,' Daniel said, kissing his son goodbye.

Even though he knew their son would be perfectly safe with Jenny, that Jordan treated Iain as if he were his own flesh and blood, and Daniel himself had plans for a romantic weekend away with Beatrice, it was still a wrench to say goodbye to Iain. And Daniel lingered for a last glance of his boy as Iain trotted in through his classroom door, chattering away to his friends.

He walked back to his flat to pick up his car, then drove to Beatrice's. Funny, this weekend had been a last-minute decision, but everything had worked out perfectly. And he was really looking forward to spending time with Beatrice. Walking hand in hand with her at the edge of the sea in starlight.

It felt as if they'd known each other for much longer than two months. And it was years since he'd felt this light of spirit. He liked just being with her; she made the world feel full of sunshine.

Iain adored her, too. A couple of times over half term, Beatrice had met them after an early shift and they'd gone to the park and then out for pizza. And there had been a Sunday morning where Beatrice had refused to tell them where they were going, claiming it was a surprise, and then had presented them with tickets for the children's show at the Planetarium in Greenwich. Iain had been ecstatic—he loved outer space as much as he loved football—and he'd held Beatrice's hand all the way through the show and chattered excitedly to her over lunch about the stars and the planets and the big bear in the sky. She'd been patient with him and helped him draw pictures of constellations that he'd taken into school the next day for show and tell. And when Daniel watched them together he was pretty sure that Iain's feelings towards Beatrice were very much mutual.

They'd insisted that Beatrice was just Dad's friend from work, including when Susan had joined them for pizza. But Daniel's mother had said quietly to him afterwards, 'You don't look at each other like friends.'

No. If he was honest with himself, Daniel didn't think of her as just a friend. But he wasn't ready to declare himself just yet. It was still early days. They were taking things slowly, carefully; they'd both been through a lot in the past, and there was Iain to consider. But he was really looking forward to spending the whole weekend with her.

On the way to Beatrice's, his phone pinged to signal an incoming text. Probably something last-minute from Jenny or his mother, he thought. He'd pick up the message later.

But, when he got to Beatrice's, her car wasn't parked where it usually was. And when he rang her doorbell there was no answer.

Maybe she'd nipped to the shop for something she'd forgotten. Though the woman he worked with in the Emergency Department was incredibly organised, and he couldn't imagine her forgetting anything or running out of anything. Maybe that text was from her, then, to warn him that she'd had to go out briefly and would be back any second. He took his phone from his pocket and glanced at the screen.

The message was indeed from Beatrice, but it was the last thing he'd expected.

Sorry. Can't make Cornwall. Will call you later.

What did she mean, she couldn't make Cornwall? They'd planned the trip together. He'd found a gorgeous hotel situated right next to a beach. They were going to paddle in the sea, walk for miles on the sand, and eat way too many scones with jam and clotted cream.

The only thing he could think of was that there had been an emergency in her family. A sudden illness, perhaps, or an accident. But surely she would've called him on her way out, or at least added a couple of words of explanation of her text? Beatrice was a very clear communicator at work; in the emergency room, everyone knew exactly what their role was and what she expected of them. This text raised way more questions than it answered—and it wasn't like the woman he'd got to know over the last couple of months.

It didn't make sense.

Frowning, he called her.

'The number you are calling is not contactable. Please try later or send a text,' a recorded voice informed him, and he cut the connection.

They were in London, so it was unlikely that she was out of signal range; and, like him, if she was driving she connected her phone to the car's hands-free system. For that voicemail message to kick in, she must have switched off her phone. Given that she must've known he'd call her as soon as he picked up her text, it was looking as if she really didn't want to talk to him.

Why?

They hadn't had a fight, and he couldn't think of anything he might have done that would upset her.

Puzzled and hurt, he called her again, and this time he left a message on her voicemail. 'Beatrice, it's Daniel. Are you OK? Whatever's happened, is there anything I can do? Give me a call when you can.'

Home.

Seeing the house with its four square turrets and the copper-roofed cupola made Beatrice feel slightly less panicky. When she got to the black iron gates of the rear entrance the family used, she hopped out of the car and punched in the security number. The gate swung open without so much as a creak; she drove through, waited for them to close behind her, then drove down to the house and parked on the gravel next to her sister-in-law Vicky's four-by-four.

The house wasn't open to the public until the afternoon, so she didn't have to worry about visitors. She just let herself in through the side entrance and walked into the family kitchen.

'Bea! I didn't know you were coming this weekend or I would've made sure your bed was aired. The kettle's hot,' Vicky said. 'Sandy's out doing farm stuff and Orlando's somewhere with Pa, and Ma and Flora have gone dress-shopping.'

'And you thought you were going to have a morning of peace and quiet?' Beatrice asked.

'Considering this miscreant ate Henry's school shoes and then threw them up everywhere,' Vicky said, gesturing to the black Labrador whose nose was poking out from under the table, 'I didn't get the P and Q anyway.' Vicky gave her a hug. 'So why didn't you say you were coming? I could've got something nice in for lunch. You'll have to slum it with a cheese sandwich, or go and sweet-talk them in the café—oh, my days.' Vicky patted Beatrice's arm, seeing the fat tear rolling down her face.

'Sorry. I'll pull myself together in a second.'

'What's happened, Bea? Something at work? I'll make you that cup of tea.'

Beatrice could see the alarm on her sister-in-law's face. 'Vicky, it's all right. You're not going to knock on my door later and not get an answer. And you don't have to lock up all the paracetamol in the medicine cabinet. I'm not going to take another overdose.'

'Good.' Vicky blew out a breath of sheer relief. 'I— Look, you know we're all useless at wobbly stuff, and I don't know what to say to make anything better, but if you want to talk…' She delved in the cupboard. 'Banana bread. There's a new boy in Henry's class who's dairy intolerant, so I've been trying a few things before he comes over for supper. You can be my guinea pig.'

Cake and a cup of tea was Vicky's standard answer to any problem, Beatrice knew.

'You,' she said, 'are a total sweetie. Cake and a cup of tea sounds perfect.'

The fear went from Vicky's expression, and she bustled around, organising tea and cake.

When they were sitting at the kitchen table with mugs of tea, and Cerberus had plonked himself on Beatrice's feet to comfort her, Vicky reached across and squeezed Beatrice's hand. Beatrice knew this was her sister-in-law's way of saying she was ready to listen.

There wasn't any way she could think of to soften the news, so she came straight out with it. 'I'm pregnant.'

Vicky almost dropped her mug. 'What? But—how?'

'You've got two children, Vicky. I think you know how babies are made,' Beatrice said with a smile.

'Well, of course, What I mean is—I didn't know you were even dating.' Vicky's eyes widened. 'How far along are you? How long have you been seeing him? And have you told him?'

Beatrice sighed. 'We've been seeing each other for a few weeks, I'm two weeks late and I did the test today. And, no, I haven't told him. It's complicated.'

'Because of Taylor?'

'Partly. Plus we work together. Daniel's a single dad.'

'Ah. Does his child like you?'

'Iain?' Beatrice couldn't help smiling when she thought of him. 'Yes. He's four. He wants to be a footballer and an astronaut, he thinks I'm a princess, and he also says I make the best chocolate brownies in the world.'

'Beresford brownies?'

'Of course Beresford brownies,' Beatrice confirmed.

'So what's he like?' Vicky asked. 'Daniel, I mean.'

'He's nice. He's a good doctor, he's kind and he's thorough.'

Vicky rolled her eyes. 'I don't mean at work. I mean the man himself.'

'Tall, dark and handsome. He has the most amazing dark eyes. He's sweet and he's funny. He makes me feel like a teenager, holding hands in the back row of the cinema. We talk every night on a video call after Iain's gone to bed.' She smiled. 'And we went to Notting Hill.'

'So you'd seen him the day you brought me those gorgeous Staffordshire dogs?' Vicky asked thoughtfully.

Beatrice nodded. 'Thinking back, that might have been the weekend *this* happened.'

'You were glowing, Bea. I haven't seen you look like that since…' Vicky let the words tail off.

'Since before Taylor,' Beatrice finished. 'He makes me feel lighter of spirit.'

'Do you love him?'

Beatrice wrinkled her nose. 'We've been dating for six weeks. How can I be in love?'

'OK, let's scale back. Do you like him?'

'Yes. A lot.' But love…? She wasn't sure she was ready to say that.

'Ignore the baby for now, but imagine life without him. Would there be a hole?' Vicky asked.

Beatrice didn't even have to think about it. 'A big one,' she admitted.

'Well, then. There's your answer. Call it any name you like, but you love him.' Vicky paused. 'Does he love you?'

'We haven't discussed it.'

Vicky frowned. 'OK. Does he know about Taylor? And…?'

'The overdose? Yes.'

'Then what's the issue?' Vicky asked. 'He knows what happened to you—so you must really trust him to have told him. He's already a dad so, if he's got custody, he must be a really good dad. Is he a widower?'

'Divorced. Iain stays with his mum every other weekend—like this one. Daniel and I were meant to be going away.'

'As you're here, clearly you called it off.'

Beatrice winced. 'By text.'

'Oh, *Bea*. You can't do that to the poor man.'

'I know.' Beatrice squirmed. 'I'm a cow. But I did the test and I panicked. I can't go away with him, knowing I'm pregnant and knowing that he has no idea.'

'Then tell him about the baby. He's a doctor, so he knows how babies are made.' Vicky threw Beatrice's words back at her.

'I don't know how he's going to react.'

'He's close to his little boy, yes?' At Beatrice's nod, Vicky continued, 'Then my guess is he'll be pleased. Shocked at first, especially as you haven't been together that long, but when he thinks about it he'll be pleased.'

Beatrice wasn't so sure. 'It's complicated,' she said again.

'It's not going to be an easy conversation, but you're better at talking than the rest of us put together,' Vicky said. 'And remember the family motto.'

The one carved into the dining room fireplace. *Tenacitas per aspera*. Strength through adversity.

'Strictly in confidence—' and Beatrice knew Vicky wouldn't say a word to anyone '—Iain's mum had postnatal depression. Badly. She left the baby and disappeared for a couple of days,' Beatrice said.

'Ah.' Vicky grimaced. 'One step down from what you did.'

Beatrice nodded. 'And she's pregnant again now. Daniel's panicking that Iain's going to get hurt. And now on top of this there's me. How can I tell him?'

'You're right. It's complicated,' Vicky said, 'but running away here—which isn't that far from what his ex did—isn't going to solve anything.'

'I know.' She was fast becoming Daniel's nightmare re-personified. 'What am I going to do, Vicky?'

'I guess we start with the tough one. Do you want the baby?'

Which, right now, was a collection of

cells. Beatrice rested her hand on her abdomen. 'I lost Taylor. Pregnancy scares me stupid. The idea of something going wrong and losing another baby...' She blew out a breath. 'I don't want a termination.'

'So that's the big decision made,' Vicky said. 'If Daniel doesn't want to be involved, we'll support you.'

Beatrice felt tears pricking her eyelids. 'Oh, Vicky.'

'Of course we'd support you, Bea. I know how hard it was for you when I had George. Every time I took him to postnatal class or toddler group or anything, I kept thinking about how you and Taylor should've been there with me. It was miserable for me, so it must have been hell on earth for you.'

'I have good days and bad days,' Beatrice said.

'Call him. Talk to him,' Vicky advised. 'Dragging your feet about it won't achieve anything. I don't know him so I have no idea how he'll react. But there's only one way to find out.'

'I know. And thank you.' Beatrice stood up, walked round the table and hugged her. 'You're a lot better at wobbly stuff than you give yourself credit for.'

'Hmm. Stop wriggling out of it and call him,' Vicky said.

Beatrice took her phone from her bag and switched it on. 'Oh. There's a voicemail.' She listened to it and swallowed hard. 'Oh, God. I sent him that text saying I couldn't go to Cornwall with him and I didn't even make a feeble excuse. And he hasn't left me an angry message asking what the hell I'm playing at—he's just asked me if I'm all right and if there's anything he can do.'

'A man who didn't love you would be furious. He's putting you first,' Vicky said thoughtfully. 'That makes him a keeper. Look, I'm going to take this vile hound out to do this business—and why Orlando had to leave him with me this morning I have no idea—so you go ahead and call him.'

Daniel's phone shrilled and he looked at the screen.

Beatrice.

He answered swiftly. 'Beatrice? Are you all right?'

'Yes.' She paused. 'I'm sorry, Daniel. I haven't been fair to you. And I'll pay for the hotel.'

'It doesn't matter about the hotel,' he said.

'As long as you're all right. What's happened? Where are you?'

'At Beresford,' she said.

So he'd guessed right and it was a family emergency. 'Something's happened to your family? Is there anything I can do?'

'They're all fine,' she said. 'Daniel, we need to talk.'

His stomach swooped. Had she left because she'd realised she didn't want to be with him after all, and she'd wanted space to find the right way to tell him? Just like Jenny had walked out on him, and their marriage had fizzled out after her postnatal depression? 'OK,' he said carefully.

'Would you mind coming here? Nearly everyone's out—there's just my sister-in-law Vicky at the house, so we can have some privacy.'

She wanted him to drive all the way out to her family home so she could dump him? Hurt lashed through him. 'Just give it to me straight,' he said. 'Actually, no, I'll save you the trouble. I come with complications and you'd rather keep this thing between us strictly professional, right?'

'It's not that at all,' she said. 'We need to

talk. Please, Daniel. Or I could come back to London, if you'd rather.'

If she didn't want to break up with him, what did she want to talk to him about? And if there wasn't an emergency at her family home, why had she rushed there and cancelled her weekend?

'What aren't you telling me?' he asked.

'Something I need to discuss with you face to face. I find talking hard, Daniel, and this isn't something I can do over the phone.'

Reluctantly, he said, 'OK, I'll come to you.'

She gave him the postcode for his satnav. 'Let me know when you're ten minutes away and I'll walk down to the gate and let you in.'

'Tradesmen's entrance?' he asked, knowing it was nasty but not being able to stop himself lashing out. She'd hurt him. He didn't have a clue what was going on in her head.

'Family private entrance, rather than the one we use for visitors with the public car park,' she corrected, and he felt small.

'Sorry,' he muttered.

'I'm sorry, too,' she said. 'I'll see you in a bit.'

Beresford Castle was almost an hour's

drive away. As Beatrice had asked, he called her when he was ten minutes away.

'Thank you for coming, Daniel.' She sounded cool and calm, completely in control of herself. 'I'll walk down to the gate.'

It was a ten-minute walk from the house to the gate?

Then again, she was the daughter of a viscount. The house was open to the public, so it must be enormous.

As he drove past the front entrance, he discovered that the castle was even bigger than he expected. It wasn't like a child's storybook castle: more like a mansion, with a square turret at each corner, a parapet, and a dome with a green copper roof on the top.

He was way, way out of his league.

And he didn't have a clue what Beatrice wanted to talk to him about. What was so important that it would make her cancel their weekend only minutes before they were due to leave, and she couldn't talk to him on the phone about it?

She'd implied she wasn't dumping him— but had he got it wrong?

There was only one way to find out.

CHAPTER TEN

WHEN BEATRICE MET Daniel by the unassuming wrought iron gates, she looked cool and calm and completely at home. Well, of course she would, he thought, cross with himself for being stupid. She was the viscount's daughter and she'd grown up here.

'Hi,' she said.

Her expression was carefully masked. He didn't have a clue what was going on in her head. Or what to do. Should he get out of the car, the way he wanted to, and take her in his arms? Or would she back away, preferring him to keep his distance?

Then he noticed the black Labrador by her heels.

'Yours?' he asked.

'My brother Orlando's,' she explained. The one whose children had Greek names—

and so did his dog, Daniel remembered. 'Cerberus.'

The Labrador wagged his tail politely at the sound of his name.

'Fortunately this one has only one head. He's in disgrace for chomping Henry's school shoes this morning and then being sick everywhere,' she said brightly.

'Uh-huh.' This was slightly surreal. Beatrice was talking to him—but she wasn't talking about whatever had made her flee from London to here. He might as well be a million miles away.

'Welcome to Hades,' she said.

He frowned. She'd come straight here. Why would she be here if she hated the place? 'I thought you loved your family home?'

'I do. I meant me,' she said.

She saw *herself* as Hades? But why would she be his idea of hell? He really didn't understand. 'Are you getting in?' he asked when she'd closed the gate behind them.

'Do you mind if Cerberus comes in the back of your car? For once, he's not muddy—but he might shed a few hairs.'

'I can live with dog hairs. I'm here because you wanted to talk,' he reminded her.

'We'll talk at the house.'

And her tone was so determined that he knew it was pointless arguing and trying to get her to put him out of his misery right here and right now. The quicker he drove them to the house, the quicker she'd tell him what was going on. Though he couldn't help feeling hurt. He'd driven here all the way from London, because she'd asked him to. Right now, she was all efficient and professional, the way she was in the emergency room; there was none of the warmth and sweetness of the woman he knew outside work.

She let the dog into the back of the car, where he lay down on the seat and behaved impeccably, then she got into the passenger seat.

'Where shall I park?' he asked as she directed him to the back of the house.

'Anywhere on the gravel. Next to me would be fine.'

He parked the car; she climbed out and let the dog out of the back, and Cerberus trotted over to a door and sat patiently staring at it.

'The kitchen. He's probably going to try scrounging banana bread from Vicky,' she said. 'Would you like some? It's almost lunchtime, so you must be starving.'

Daniel's stomach was rumbling, but he ignored it. He'd had enough of Beatrice's politeness. 'I'd rather know what's going on,' he said.

'Fair enough.' She opened the door, and ushered him inside. 'Oh. Vicky must've gone somewhere,' she said, sounding surprised that her sister-in-law wasn't in the kitchen. 'Cerberus, you bad hound, on your bed. You know you're not allowed in the main house until the evening.'

The Labrador gave her a mournful look, but went over to a larger wicker basket and threw himself down on the cushions with a dramatic sigh, then lay with his nose on his paws.

'This way,' she said to Daniel, and led him through to the main part of the house. The grand entrance hall had a chequered marble floor and oak panelling. There was a very fancy grandfather clock in one corner, cabinets with inlaid marquetry, and what looked like some kind of weighing machine. There were also enormous oil paintings on the wall, all with ornate gilt frames, and Venetian glass chandeliers hung from the ceiling.

It felt more like a film set than a home. One of those Jane Austen comedy of manners films that Jenny had loved, but had annoyed him because he hated all the snobbishness.

This didn't bode well.

In silence, he followed her up the wide curving staircase, through corridors lined with more of the huge oil paintings—portraits of Lindford ancestors, he guessed— up more stairs, and finally up a spiral stone staircase.

When they got to the top and she led him out of a narrow wooden door, he realised they were standing on the roof of the house. 'I wasn't expecting this.'

'The view's pretty amazing from up here.'

'It is,' he agreed.

'But that isn't why I brought you here. This is.' She gestured to the cupola. 'My Great-great-uncle Sebastian's observatory.'

She opened the door and switched on the light. 'There are two lights. The red light's for night-time when it's being used as a proper observatory, and obviously this one is for daytime.'

The walls inside were wooden-panelled; there was a shelf of what looked like books on astronomy, and the ceiling of the dome was painted like an old star map, complete with mythological creatures. In the centre of the room was a large mounted telescope. It was absolutely amazing. 'Iain would be beside himself with excitement if he saw this.'

'And I'm looking forward to showing him,' she said.

But—wasn't she trying to dump him? Why would she suggest bringing Iain here if she was going to split up with him?

'My great-great-uncle turned the cupola into an observatory when he came back here after the First World War, so he could sit up here and watch the stars. I guess it was his way of coping with shell shock,' Beatrice said.

'PTSD, as we know it now,' Daniel said.

'It's a good place to think. Just you and the sky. Especially after midnight, when the only lights here are security lights that switch on if they detect movement—otherwise it's miles and miles to the nearest street lamps, so the skies are incredible.' She pressed a lever, and a slice of the roof slid open. 'The roof of the dome rotates—there's another switch for that—so you can move it with the telescope to see whatever you want, at any time of year.'

Then he realised why she'd brought him here. This was obviously her safe place, the way it had been for her great-great-uncle. Her place to think. 'Is this where you came to sit after you lost Taylor?' he asked.

'Yes. Looking up at the stars was the only thing that made any sense, for a while. I got to understand Sebastian very, very well.' She looked at him. 'I'm sorry, Daniel. I haven't been fair to you.'

'I'm sure you had your reasons.' He held her gaze. 'Though I would appreciate an explanation. Right now I don't have a clue what's happening. And, if I'm being honest, I'm a bit hurt that you didn't even give me a reason—you just left.'

'I'm sorry,' she said again. 'I've been trying to find the right words. I'm still trying. And I just don't know how to say it.'

So was she dumping him or not? 'Keep it simple,' he said. 'That's usually the best way, even when you think it's complicated.'

'Oh, it's complicated, all right,' she said. 'I can't think of a way to soften it, so I'll try it your way. Forgive me, because this is going to be a bit of a shock.' She swallowed hard. 'I'm pregnant.'

He stared at her, not sure that he'd really heard her correctly. 'Pregnant?' he repeated.

'Pregnant,' she said again.

It felt as if someone had just dropped him from a great height into the middle of the sea. His ears were roaring and he couldn't breathe. Pregnant? But she couldn't be. They'd been careful. They hadn't taken a single risk.

OK, so there was a tiny, tiny—infinitesimally tiny—chance that a condom wouldn't prevent a pregnancy. A chance so small that he hadn't really considered it to be a risk at all. They were both over thirty, her fertility levels were dropping by the day, and all the unexpected pregnancies he'd ever heard about were due to taking risks.

But that tiny, tiny chance had resulted in a baby.

'I'm sorry.' She looked anguished.

'It's not your fault. It takes two to make a baby.'

'I don't mean that. I mean I'm sorry for giving you this news just after Jenny dropped her bombshell. I know this is your worst nightmare.'

Now he began to understand what she'd meant about 'welcome to Hades'. She'd known she was about to resurrect the past for him. Jenny, the postnatal depression, the way Jenny had walked out and left Iain. He'd been very sure that he didn't want to take that risk ever again and have another child.

But she'd also been very clear that she didn't want a child. That she couldn't face the possibility of things going wrong again and losing a baby the same way she'd lost her daughter. 'It's your worst nightmare, too.' He looked at her. 'So how pregnant are you? When did you find out?'

'My period's two weeks late,' she said. 'I guess with all that's been happening, I haven't really been thinking about my cycle. But I've been regular as clockwork for years and years. The only time I missed a period was when I was pregnant with Taylor. And this morning when I got up I felt odd—like I did the last time I was pregnant. When I counted back to my last period and I realised I was late, it was the obvious answer. I kept trying to tell myself that I was being ridiculous and I went through every single medical reason for missing a period, the vast majority of which didn't apply to me.' She grimaced. 'So I bought a test. Just to prove to myself that we'd been careful and of course I wasn't pregnant. Except the test was positive—and then I panicked.'

And she'd fled to her safe place. Here.

'I know you don't want another child,' she said.

'You said you didn't, either.' He paused, trying to work this out. 'So if you count back to your LMP, that makes you six weeks.'

'And I'm scared,' she said softly. 'Not just about whether I'm going to be able to carry a baby to term or if I'm going to have an abruption.'

'What else are you scared about?'

'Honestly? I don't know how this is going to work out. We haven't been seeing each other for very long.'

Then the penny dropped. She hadn't brought him here to dump him—she'd asked him to come here because she thought *he* was going to dump *her* when she broke the news about her pregnancy, and she wanted to be here to lick her wounds.

'Put it this way, you're the first woman I've dated since my marriage broke up,' he said. 'The first in four years. Which I think counts for something.'

'It's the same for me. You're the first man I've dated since my marriage broke up,' she echoed. 'The first in four years.'

'Which I think also counts for something,' he said. The fact that they'd taken a risk on each other, when both of them were so wary about relationships.

'Maybe. But none of this was supposed to happen.' She spread her hands. 'We were supposed to be seeing where this took us. Taking it slowly.'

'Maybe it's just happened a little faster than we intended,' he said wryly.

'Faster? I'm pregnant,' she said. 'That's so fast it's almost supersonic. And this is your worst nightmare. You're worried enough about Jenny's new pregnancy and what effect it might have on Iain; and you know I had mental health issues after my baby died. That I took an overdose. Doesn't that make me too risky to be around Iain?'

'It happened years ago. You're in a different place now. And what you suggested about Jenny applies to you, too,' he pointed out. 'If your health professionals know about your history and they're keeping an eye on you, and if you have the right support at home...' He let the words tail off, and sighed. 'I let Jenny down. I didn't give her the right support. Who's to say I won't let you down, too?'

'For what it's worth, I know you weren't deliberately unsupportive. Everyone missed the signs.' She looked him straight in the eye. 'You're not the kind of man to let someone down.'

She had rather more faith in him than he did in himself, he thought.

'So where does this leave us?' she asked.

'Honestly? I don't have a clue. I've just found out that you're pregnant. I'm still trying to get my head round that,' he said. 'A baby.'

'Believe me, I've only had a couple more hours than you to get my head round it,' she said.

'And have you managed it?'

She grimaced. 'Yes and no. I talked to Vicky.'

'What did she say?'

'She was better than she thought at the wobbly stuff,' Beatrice said. 'Though she was a bit brutal. She asked me if I wanted a termination.'

'That's one option,' he said, striving to keep his tone non-judgemental. It was an option that didn't sit well with him; if there were medical reasons for a termination, if the mum's life was at stake, then fair enough. But to get rid of a baby just because it wasn't convenient… To him, that felt wrong.

'It's not an option for me,' she said. 'I lost a baby at twenty-eight weeks, Daniel. Yes, I know that right now our baby could be considered as little more than a collection of cells, but I just can't…' She blew out a breath. 'I told her no.'

'I'm glad,' he said. 'Because that's how I feel.'

'OK. So we're agreed that we're keeping the baby. That leads us to the next decision we have to make,' she said. 'Do we raise the child together, or will I be a single parent?'

'You and me. A family,' he said. 'We could do that.'

'There's not just us to consider,' she said.

He could have kissed her for that; it told him that she wasn't going to push Iain away.

'How would Iain feel about it? About us all living together, about the baby?'

'Iain hasn't stopped talking about you since you fixed his arm on the football field. I don't know if it's that, the fact you play trains with him, your brownies, or that amazing day out you organised at the Planetarium—he adores you and he's forever asking me when we can see you next,' Daniel said. 'I think I can safely say he'd be happy about it. But, I warn you, if you live with us you'll have to put up with hours and hours of questions from him.'

'He's bright.' She smiled. 'He'll come up with interesting questions. I'll enjoy that.'

'On a Friday night, when I'm tired and I can't think of answers, it'll be nice to have someone else to come up with suggestions.' He paused. 'So how about you? Is that what you want?'

'All I can think about right now,' she admitted, 'is how scared I am that everything's going to go wrong.'

'There's a fairly big part of my head doing the same right now,' he said. 'But then I think of my little boy. Things *did* go wrong for us, but we've muddled through and we're doing OK.'

She swallowed hard. 'My situation didn't have an option for muddling through.'

'What happened to you,' he said softly, 'was terrible. I'm sorry you lost the baby, and I'm sorry that you were so low you didn't want to be in this world any more. But there's an inner strength to you, Beatrice. You got through it. And you know what we said about this being our second chance?'

She said nothing, but he could see a spark of hope in the fear in her beautiful blue eyes. And he wanted to fan that hope into a proper flame. 'Maybe this baby is part of that second chance. Yes, we both have fears—even though we're doctors and we know the risks are small, we're human so of course we're going to worry that the past will repeat itself—that you'll have an abruption, putting the baby at risk, and that I won't spot any signs of postnatal depression and I'll let you down. But we can talk about our fears instead of shutting them away inside, and then they'll lose their power to hurt us.'

The hope in her eyes brightened and then dimmed again. 'I let you down. I knew what had happened with Jenny, and I shouldn't have just walked out on you. I should've at least told you that I'd come here.'

'You said yourself that you panicked. If I put myself in your shoes—well, maybe I would've done the same thing,' he said. 'And at least you called me a couple of hours later. You didn't let it get to the stage where I had people looking for you, worried sick that something had happened.'

'I was so looking forward to going away with you,' she said. 'I thought it was going to be a romantic weekend where we'd spend time together and get closer. Sunshine and sand and the sound of the sea.'

'That's what I wanted, too,' he said.

'We've only known each other a few weeks. The way I saw it, we'd keep dating for a while and we'd get closer, and then maybe we'd fall in love. We'd make a family with Iain when we were ready and we'd all got used to the idea. But the baby's changed all that.'

'Has it? Maybe it's just changed the timescale a bit,' he said.

'So, what—we make a family and then hope we fall in love?'

Did that mean she didn't feel the same way about him? Or was she trying to be brave and breezy and not put any pressure on him?

If she didn't love him, he had nothing to lose.

If she did love him and she was trying to be brave because she didn't think he loved her, then he had everything to gain.

'I didn't say the order had changed, just the timescale,' he pointed out.

Her eyes went wide. 'So are you saying…?'

'I'm saying you're right, we haven't known each other for very long—but we've known each other for long enough for me to know that I love you,' he said. 'There's you at work, all kind and calm and professional. You're very easy to like. But it's not just the fact I like you. It's not just a physical thing, either, even though you're gorgeous and, as Iain says, you have hair like a princess. It's *you*. The woman who talks to me last thing at night so I go to sleep smiling. The woman who makes chocolate cake that I actually enjoy eating, and believe me I've had more than thirty years of loathing chocolate cake. The woman who dances with me in her kitchen and makes me feel as if I'm walking on air. It's you. The way you make me feel. When I'm with you I feel that I'm living, not just existing.'

'That's how I feel about you, too,' she whispered. 'That I'm living, not just existing. That there's always something to look forward to in a day, whether it's a walk in the park or talking to you on the phone before I go to sleep, or drinking Prosecco in the sunset on my patio. I like being with you.' Her eyes filled with tears. 'And I hurt you today. I was a coward. Instead of talking to you, I ran away—just like Jenny did. I hurt you.'

'Yes, you did.' It was only fair to acknowledge it, now they were being honest with each other. 'But I understand why.' He paused. 'And you could always try kissing me better.'

'I could.'

The flicker of hope in her eyes was now the blaze he'd wanted it to be. He opened his arms, and she stepped into them.

And then she kissed him.

It was slow and sweet at first, even a little shy. But then he let her deepen the kiss and he wrapped his arms tightly round her. This was where he wanted to be. With her. Holding her. Loving her. Being part of her life.

When she broke the kiss, they were both shaking.

'I love you, too, Daniel,' she said. 'And I want to be a family with you. The two of us, Iain and our baby. And the extended family—I like your mum, and I think you'll get on just fine with my lot. I'd like to be friends with Jenny, so she'll know she's always welcome in your life. And it really doesn't matter whether we get married or not, as long as we're together.' She stroked her face. 'But I think we shouldn't move in together until we're sure that Iain's happy with the situation. That he knows you're still his dad; that although I'm not his biological mum and I'd never try to push Jenny out, I'd like him to think of me as his other mum; and that he's going to have another little brother or sister to boss around.'

'Agreed,' he said.

'And,' she added, 'I'm going to try and push past all the fears. I don't want our pasts to get in the way of our future and I know you'll have my back—just as I'll have yours.'

'Always,' he said, and kissed her.

EPILOGUE

A year later

'THE PLANETARIUM?' BEATRICE ASKED. 'I love it here, darling, but I'm not sure your baby brother's quite old enough to come here.'

'But, Mum,' Iain said plaintively, 'it's my favourite place—well, except Great-great-great-uncle Sebastian's observatory on Grampa's roof, and maybe the park if we're playing football.'

'Let's do the park and play football today, and then we can come to the Planetarium another day, when one of your grandmothers or your mum can look after Rowan for us,' Beatrice suggested.

Iain shook his head. 'But he'll love it, Mum. He loves the starry sky lights I chose him.'

The light show that played constellations,

the moon and the sun over the ceiling. They'd chosen it together after the twenty-week scan—which Iain had come to with them, and had been convinced that his new baby brother had waved to him, so Iain had been adamant that the starry sky light should be his 'welcome to the world' present to his baby brother.

'He might start crying in the middle of the show,' Beatrice said gently, 'and that isn't fair to all the other people who came to see it.'

'But we *have* to go,' Iain said, hopping from foot to foot. 'Tell, her, Dad!'

'I'm with Iain. My vote's for the Planetarium today,' Daniel said with a smile.

She was all for the father-son bond, but the pair of them really hadn't thought this through properly. 'What if Rowan starts crying in the middle of the show?' Beatrice asked again.

Daniel coughed and indicated the fast asleep baby in the pram he was pushing. 'I'm pretty sure he's out for the count.'

'He might wake up.'

'*Mum*. It's our special place because we live in London and we can't always go to Great-great-great-uncle Sebastian's observatory,' Iain said. 'I know he'll love it there. Please.'

Daniel produced an envelope from his back pocket. 'We've got VIP tickets, as it's Rowan's first time at the Planetarium.'

'Oh, for goodness' sake. You've got more money than sense,' Beatrice said, rolling her eyes. 'And if your son does start crying in the middle of the show, Daniel Capaldi, you'll be the one taking him out and checking his nappy.' She put her hands on her hips and stared at Iain. 'And you'll be going with your dad, Iain Capaldi, to hold the nappy bag. And if it's a really stinky one, it'll serve you both right.' But her indignation was mostly for show. She loved Iain's enthusiasm for the stars, she loved the fact that he'd wanted to call her 'Mum' as well as Jenny—with Jenny's blessing—and she loved the fact he wanted to share everything with his new baby brother.

Life with her new family was pretty much perfect. Although she and Daniel had worried about the pregnancy and what would happen afterwards, her maternity team had kept a close eye on her throughout the pregnancy and reassured them both. She'd flinched every time she'd got behind the wheel of the car in her twenty-eighth week, but she'd made herself drive to help her put the past behind her, and Daniel had been there to reassure her that everything would be just fine. And it had been; she got to the twenty-ninth week, and finally she could put the fears behind her.

Everything had gone smoothly for the rest of her pregnancy, and Rowan had decided to make his appearance on his actual due date rather than surprising them early or making them wait longer.

After Rowan's birth, it had been Daniel's turn to be twitchy and Beatrice's turn to reassure him. As the days passed and she hadn't shown any sign of postnatal depression, he'd begun to relax. Now Rowan was three months old, happy and healthy; they'd moved from Daniel's flat to a house with a garden and the potential promise of getting a rescue dog. And the world felt full of sunshine.

The auditorium was remarkably empty, Beatrice thought as they made their way inside. 'Are we super-early for the show?' she asked Daniel as they took their seats—ones she'd chosen as near to the door as possible, so they could make a quick and quiet exit with the baby if they needed to.

'No, we're right on time,' Daniel said.

'But nobody else is here.'

'We've got VIP tickets, Mum,' Iain reminded her. 'Especially for Rowan's first show.'

Which the baby was sleeping through quite contentedly, Beatrice thought wryly. 'OK,' she said. Maybe Daniel had booked a short private viewing for the four of them—though surely he would've said that rather than telling her that they had VIP tickets?

A man she assumed was that session's astronomer took the stage. 'Today's showing is a special tour of our solar system,' he said. 'Starting with a flight through Saturn's rings.'

That was an odd choice, Beatrice thought. She would've expected him to start either with Neptune, the furthest out, and work inwards; or the sun itself and work outwards.

The lights dimmed and music began playing. As the first pictures of Saturn came into view, the astronomer left the stage.

That was odd, too, Beatrice thought. The astronomer usually stood to the side of the stage and talked everyone through what they were seeing.

Even odder was that Iain and Daniel both quietly got up and walked towards the stage.

She was about to protest and call them back to their seats when the picture changed, becoming static rather than a video of Saturn and its rings. The picture was still Saturn, but there was a message written on the planet's rings in bright pink lettering.

Beatrice Lindford, will you marry us?

The lights came up to reveal Daniel and Iain on the stage, both of them kneeling on one knee in the traditional pose.

'Mum, we love you to the end of the universe and back,' Iain said.

Daniel opened his hand to reveal a velvet-covered box with a solitaire diamond ring nestling in it. 'For the last year, since you moved in with us, you've made us both so happy. And now we've got Rowan, too.'

'You're the only one in the house who isn't a Capaldi, and you *need* to be a Capaldi,' Iain added.

'So will you marry us?' Daniel asked.

Beatrice blinked away the tears, checked

that Rowan was still fast asleep, then walked over to the stage to join them—the man she loved and the little boy she loved as if he was her own. 'Yes,' she said. 'Most definitely yes.'

Daniel slid the ring onto her finger and kissed her thoroughly. Iain, meanwhile, was busy using Daniel's phone. And then Daniel's phone pinged to signal an incoming text.

'I'll get it, Dad.' Iain peered at the screen.

'All OK, son?' Daniel asked.

'Yup.' Iain was grinning his head off, clearly delighted about something.

But Beatrice didn't have a chance to ask what her menfolk were plotting, because Daniel said, 'Our slot's about to finish. Let's go out this way and we'll go and get a cup of tea to celebrate.'

'And cake,' Iain said. 'It won't be as good as your cake, Mum, but almost.'

'Tea and cake it is,' Beatrice agreed. She followed them out of the door, only to be greeted with a barrage of party poppers and loud cheering.

It took her a moment or two to realise what was going on—but then she saw that all their family was there. Her parents, her brothers and sisters-in-law, her niece and nephews, Daniel's mum and his grandparents, Jenny and Jordan and their new baby girl. There was also a fair sprinkling of their friends outside work, along with everyone from their department who wasn't on duty. 'I can't believe everyone's here!'

'It's not every day you get engaged. And you can't have an engagement without a party,' Daniel said, looking very pleased with himself.

'But—how did you manage to get everyone here?' she asked.

'We asked them,' Iain said, looking even more pleased with himself than his father did.

'You both arranged this whole party on your own?' The room was decorated, there was food and drink, there was music, there were balloons… Everything was perfect.

'We had a bit of help,' Daniel admitted. 'Our mums and Vicky organised the invitations and did all the booking, so you wouldn't accidentally see an email or anything.'

'So everyone knew except me?' She was amazed that they'd managed to organise everything without her knowledge and that everyone had kept it secret—especially Iain, who was still young enough to blurt things out and frequently did so.

'It was *really* hard not telling you,' Iain said, 'and I nearly told you three times, but Dad said you'd be so happy if we surprised you that your eyes would go all shiny, like when I called you "Mum" the first time and when Rowan was born.'

'I *am* happy, darling.' Beatrice hugged him. 'You and Dad and Vicky and the grannies have done a wonderful job. Look at all those balloons. Oh, and the cake!'

'Vicky made the cake,' Iain said. 'She put Saturn on it.'

'That makes it even more special.' She hugged Iain again, then straightened up and turned to Daniel. 'And you are amazing.'

'I had help,' he said again. 'I really can't take very much credit for this. Our mums and Vicky were phenomenal.'

'We wanted to help because you're perfect together,' Catherine said, coming over arm in arm with Susan.

'Exactly,' Susan agreed. 'And when Daniel said he wanted to ask you to marry him somewhere special, Iain said it had to be here. We looked into it, and…' She spread her hands. 'Well, here we are. I knew when I first met you that you and Daniel were meant to be together. Welcome to the family, Bea.' She hugged Beatrice warmly.

'Welcome to the family, Daniel,' Edward said, handing him and Beatrice a glass of champagne. 'And, yes, Bea, before you say it, I know you're feeding Rowan, but a celebratory sip won't hurt.'

'Can I have some champagne, Grampa?' Iain asked.

'My little Scottish chieftain, I have something even more special for you. Let's go and find it,' Edward said, and swung Iain onto his shoulders.

'Congratulations.' Jenny hugged them in turn. 'I'm so happy for you both, And Iain's thrilled that you're officially going to be his other mum, Bea.'

'I'm thrilled, too,' Beatrice said, hugging her back.

Rowan was scooped up by his grandmothers, and Daniel held his hand out to Beatrice. 'Come and dance,' he said with a smile.

Once they were on the dance floor and they were dancing cheek to cheek, he said, 'Iain and me, we love you to the end of the universe and back.'

'That's how much I love you, too,' Beatrice said. 'And this has to be the most perfect place for you to propose and for us to get engaged. I can't believe you all set this up between you. It's fantastic. All our family and friends here to celebrate with us, and you all kept it so quiet!'

'It's going to be a very short engagement,' Daniel warned, 'because I can't wait to marry you. Besides, if we leave it too long, our young wedding planner's going to start suggesting that we get married on the moon and get everyone there by rocket.'

Beatrice laughed. 'We could always hire a film set…' She kissed him. 'I love you. And I don't mind where we get married or when, just as long as we're together.'

'Together.' He kissed her. 'Always.'

* * * * *

*If you enjoyed this story, check out
these other great reads from
Kate Hardy*

Unlocking the Italian Doc's Heart
Their Pregnancy Gift
Christmas with Her Daredevil Doc
Mommy, Nurse…Duchess?

All available now!